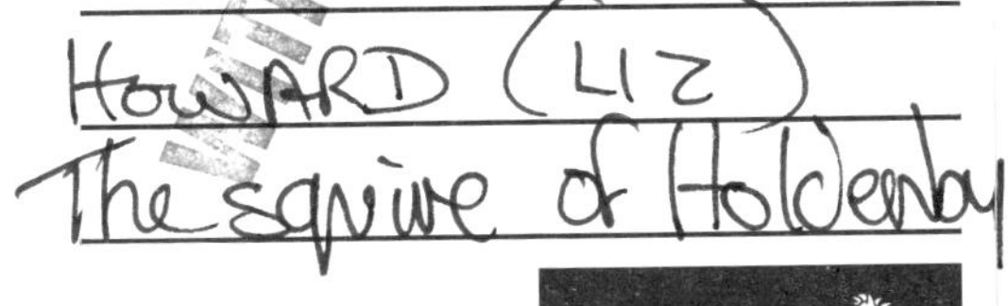
HOWARD (LIZ)
The squire of Holdenby

CHARTER MARK

Kent
County
Council

THE SQUIRE OF HOLDENBY

Liz Howard

Chivers Press
Bath, England

•

G.K. Hall & Co.
Waterville, Maine USA

This Large Print edition is published by Chivers Press, England, and by G.K. Hall & Co., USA.

Published in 2001 in the U.K. by arrangement with the author.

Published in 2001 in the U.S. by arrangement with Liz Howard.

U.K. Hardcover ISBN 0-7540-4647-8 (Chivers Large Print)
U.K. Softcover ISBN 0-7540-4648-6 (Camden Large Print)
U.S. Softcover ISBN 0-7838-9529-1 (Nightingale Series Edition)

The text of this Large Print edition is unabridged.
Other aspects of the book may vary from the original edition.

Set in 16 pt. New Times Roman.

Printed in Great Britain on acid-frce paper.

British Library Cataloguing in Publication Data available

Library of Congress Cataloging-in-Publication Data

Howard, Liz, 1942–
The Squire of Holdenby / Liz Howard.
p. cm.
ISBN 0-7838-9529-1 (lg. print : sc : alk. paper)
1. Large type books. I. Title.
PR6058.O8848 S68 2001
823'.92—dc21 2001039062

For Tim and Liz Richards
of Gawsworth Hall with
thanks for all their help
and encouragement.

CHAPTER ONE

Dank and cold, the narrow excavation stared up at him unblinkingly. Chill mustiness crept silently from its black, worm infested sides to shiver his back with icy fingers. Even the strong shafts of yellow sunlight piercing the gloom, cutting through the priest's familiar canting, were strangely empty of warmth as Kit fought to control limbs determined to tremble him into a state of palsied cowardice. It hadn't been as bad as this when Father died. Then there had been Francis to depend on. His eyes swivelled compulsively to the ornate casket. Strong, tall, handsome Francis. Sixteen years old. The brother he had worshipped and envied simultaneously for as long as he could remember. Gone. Dead. His fair skin waxen. His once laughing lips colourless. His eyes, empty.

Dorothy, standing beside him, sniffed. Kit desperately wanted to grasp her hand. To comfort her. And himself. But William Saunder's critical glance seemed to inspect him, top to toe, finding flaws in his make-up even worse than those in his puny, underdeveloped physique. His mother's brother was now his keeper absolute and with Francis, son and heir of their father, William Hatton, now being lowered into that hellish pit, attention was firmly fixed on him. The second son. Christopher Hatton. Dorothy was older, but she was a girl, so she didn't count. And Thomas, two years younger, would not yet be made to feel the harness tighten across his back. Why had Francis to die? Why . . .? He had always been the leader, and Kit the willing follower, knowing full well that he could never hope to equal, let alone better, either the brains or brawn of his idol. And now? What now?

Outside the ancient little church of Holdenby, as the farmhands and their wives drifted quietly back to their own cottages, set respectfully round the old village green on the other side of a small wood, Dorothy's fingers suddenly found the courage to entwine themselves in his.

'You'll be alright, Kit. You'll see. I just know you will.' Her own watery smile was defiantly bright as she tried not to compare this slim nine-year-old with the supple grace of her darling Francis. 'The manor, the grazing, the woods, are all yours now. All you have to do is grow. Grow as tall and strong as Francis and Uncle William will not be unkind. His bark draws more blood than his bite you know.'

William Saunders took his responsibilities seriously and consequently was often thought of as a very serious-minded man, but Dorothy had lately seen a different side to him and had been grateful for his concern in the matter of her betrothal. He had done his best for her and she thought that she would be very well suited with John Newport, respectable and moderately wealthy, from Warwickshire. Mister Saunders would be sure to do his best for Kit, and Thomas too, when the time came.

Grow as tall and strong as Francis? Could he? It didn't seem possible. But Dorothy was right. It was all his. His manor. His land. His Holdenby! The least he could do was try. Give himself a chance. He would ride. And wrestle. And tilt. Until he was as good as ever Francis had been. He would give Thomas a brother he could look up to and be proud of. A brother Dorothy could adore.

'And when I am come into my estates I shall not forget how it was my only sister who held out her hand to comfort me. Be certain of that.' Kit squeezed that hand as he turned to look out across the undulating green pastures of Northamptonshire. It was beautiful. It was home. It was his.

* * *

'Enough! Enough! I surrender!' The bones of John Messinger's elbow grated painfully together as his arm was twisted almost full circle, threatening to dislodge itself from his shoulder-joint at any second. Eyes screwed tight and lips drawn back against the pain he wretchedly listened to the laugh of triumph, waiting for the last playful jerk of victory as Kit Hatton let him go. Thank God they were friends. Young John was far from being a weakling but he would have hated to find himself face to face with Kit in a real fight. Nor would any other in the area. Mister Hatton had energy and skill enough for three and had his character shown more aggression than charm he could easily have ruled the roost by force. As it was, he was so full of fun and youthful spirit that it was impossible to dislike him.

Tom Hatton, leaning comfortably against the thick bole of the village oak, watched his brother spring to his feet and stand grinning at his vanquished friend for a moment before offering a firm hand to help him up. Was there anyone, anywhere, who could get the better of Kit? Thomas knew instinctively that he would never be his brother's equal; that he would always live his life in the shadow cast by the strong yet graceful figure of Christopher, The Squire of Holdenby.

Dusk was cautiously beginning to gather itself together beneath the trees, though the May-Eve sun still washed the spring-green grasslands with scarlet and gold. A sudden stillness descended and Tom shuddered involuntarily. Sensitive, and with the fertile imagination of a poet, he felt, almost heard, the silent approach of those spiritual twins, Destiny and Fate. The moment slid away as

Kit, cheerfully flinging his arm around John's almost dislocated shoulder and causing him to wince, turned towards him, beckoning.

'Your turn, Tom?'

The words were hardly out of his mouth when the sound of running footsteps and an excited shout had them peering through the gloom. Henry Dalton and Simon Fletcher were rushing breathlessly towards them through the woods as though their tails were on fire.

'Come up to Haddon. Now!' Henry gasped and spluttered through the words. 'It's Mary. Mary Shea.' Holding his arms around his aching ribs he panted desperately in an effort to catch his breath as it raced away from him.

'Dancing.' Simon tried to help him out. 'Around the May-Eve fire. Come on. We'll miss it.'

They'd all seen Mary Shea walk often enough. There was a spring in her step which caused her hips to sway and twitch with hypnotic fascination. Old eyes and young eyes alike found themselves glued unerringly to that provocative movement whenever Mary Shea walked by. But to watch her dance! The very idea was breathtaking!

'Come on then! Race you!' Kit Hatton was out in front before the others were half way to thinking about it.

The mysterious depths of Black Thorn Spinney threw star-burst sparks from the blazing brushwood into brilliant relief, and even at a distance Kit could make out the lissom movements of a darkened shape as it passed and repassed the flames. Faint music carried tantalizingly on the still evening air. As he grew closer his mad run reduced itself to a trot and then a walk and then a tiptoed stealth as he kept to the shadows of the hedge. The snap of twigs and the rustle of grasses told him that the others had not been long in catching him and with a swift movement of his hand he motioned them to silence. The vision before him had him mesmerized. His feet continued to inch forward. His gaze never left the whirling abandonment of the dancer for a second. The rest of the family group were merely her accessories: her father, toe-tapping as he conjured the rapid flurry of high-pitched notes from the strings with what appeared to be a magic wand, and her mother, rapping her knuckles in perfect rhythm against the tambourine. And the others. Uncles? Aunts? Cousins? Who could say? There were rumours that Mister Shea had once been a tinker, constantly on the move to make a living. Or to leave behind any trouble he had created! His temper was as wild as the unruly hair which sprang in thick, black curls from his scalp, and neither one had he ever attempted to tame. But Kit Hatton saw only the thicker, blacker curls twisting and twirling out behind the tinker's daughter as she danced to the devil's tune.

The olive tones of her skin had been transformed to burnished gold by the firelight, high cheekbones smoothly gilded, accentuating the smouldering depths of her long-lashed eyes. Full, ruby-red lips pouted sensuously in concentration as she lifted the well-worn and somewhat ragged skirt to expose her naked legs almost to the knees, revealing expertly timed intricacies of steps being performed by bare, black-soled feet.

Kit's heart was beating faster than the music, making the blood sing in his ears and causing his throat to tighten with undefined pleasure. He was hotly aware too of other, more intimate sensations flaring to attention. He felt that he could whirl into that crazy dance with her, spin around faster and faster and faster until their bodies joined and moved as one. Until they were one. Until he lost himself in her. For ever. Kit Hatton knew himself bewitched. Mary Shea danced only for him.

Then it was over. On a flourishing *crescendo* of tinkling tambourines the suppleness became frozen, almost in mid-air it seemed, before the lithe figure flung itself to its knees in a gesture of finality. And as Mary Shea raised her face to the congratulations of the audience the full impact of that free, unfettered spirit turned his knees to water and his thoughts to the morrow's Maying.

Mister Shea approached the young squire bare-headed and with signs of hospitality, a certain deference in his manner indicating that he knew his low place in the hierarchy. Tonight a touch of the forelock would not come amiss. The lad only had eyes for Mary at the moment and it would be best if they strayed no further for the time being. There were one or two trussed carcasses and several nice skins inside the croft which Shea wouldn't even think about in case Mister Hatton read his mind and had him tried as a felon.

'Ale, sir? Join us in some of my wife's fine ale.' False heartiness only served to make the tone sound more ingratiating than ever. 'We haven't much to offer, sir, but you are very welcome to sit with us as the sun sets.'

That great, glowing orb could no longer be seen but the sky was stained scarlet over the horizon, lifting to pink, then lemon, then turquoise, before smudging into the blue dome high overhead. Behind him, over dense woodland, he knew that the colour would already be deep purple as the night closed in. Kit shivered. The priest would warn him back to Holdenby and the safety of his bed. Not that these people were doing anything wrong. But May-Eve was not known as a Christian festival, and with Queen Mary setting heretics alight in both town and country it would be as well to refuse.

Mary's smile embraced him causing the

shiver to have an altogether different meaning. Oh, cock-a-snoot at the priest! This was only harmless fun and no sane man would even dream of bringing in thoughts of religion. A family party was no heathen crime, and as squire, he counted all his tenants as his family. As squire, he had every right to do as he liked. Kit stubbornly pushed aside all thoughts of William Saunders's ideas on that subject, and continued to ignore the fact that he was still some years from gaining his majority.

'Well, thank you, Mister Shea. My friends and I would not look unkindly on some small refreshment.' He only hoped that the others were not grinning like idiots behind his back.

'Mary, help your mother.' Mister Shea bowed again to Kit. 'My daughter will serve you, sir.'

The strangled sound of John Messinger trying to swallow his laughter had him blushing with annoyance, the more so as he had had that very same thought in his head since the moment he had set eyes on her tonight. Damn John Messinger! Had his feeling been so obvious?

Mary bobbed a pert curtsey before holding out the flagon, keeping her eyes lowered demurely. Only as he took the cup from her hand did she slowly raise her eyelids to startle him with an unmistakable flash of mischief. And now the smile was nothing short of inviting. In the midst of all the bustle as the others were served by Mistress Shea and ushered to rough wooden seats hurriedly set around the fire, she spoke. So softly that he barely heard.

'The dawn is best seen from the crest of Coneybury Hill.'

That was all. But by the spark of fire in her eyes he knew that he had heard aright.

Later, after the Hatton brothers and their friends had disappeared into darkness and the Sheas continued with their rituals, which seemed to depend on large quantities of ale being consumed, the head of that family had a word of caution for his daughter.

'You did well, as you've been taught, to take a man's mind off things which don't concern him, but be warned! The likes of him are not for you to tangle with. There'd be nothing in it for you but a dead babby.' No young girl abandoned by her family could have any hope of raising a child alone. And there was a sight more chance of raising a child than there was of marriage to Kit Hatton!

Mary poured more ale. Tomorrow, her father would not set eyes on the sun till noon. And by then she would have been home for hours.

* * *

The dew-laden grass licked his boots as he strode purposefully up the gentle slope. Would she be there? Or was she just a tease, laughing at his impatience from the warmth of her rough-wool bed? The pre-dawn air held a nip which went unnoticed. He had brought his cloak. But not, hot-blooded as he was, to keep himself warm. At some point during the vividly erotic dreams of a restless night, one very practical thought had struck him. The grass will be wet! Take a cloak. Treat her like a lady!

Nothing! The crest of Coneybury Hill was deserted. Echoing in solitary splendour, the first morning trill of birdsong carried effortlessly across lightening landscapes. Stomach muscles tightened uncomfortably as excitement turned to intense disappointment. He felt let down. As he had the day they buried Francis. Hesitant and uncertain. Unimportant. Unacceptable. As insecurity swamped him Kit wondered whether he would ever overcome these feelings of incompetence. Would he ever feel that he could uphold the name of Hatton as Francis would have done? Mentally thrusting the thought aside he straightened his shoulders. Why should he let a common chit like Mary Shea demoralize him like this? Who would ever know that she had made such a fool of him? No one. He wasn't going to shout it abroad, and no one else knew. Did they? But would Kit Hatton be able to forget his own stupidity? That was the problem! As he was about to start for home, he saw her. His spirit soared. His confidence returned. She had come!

He had been living for this moment through the long hours of the night, imagination playing havoc with nerve ends and his body aching with newly awakened longings which he fought desperately to repress. He never dreamed she might be shy and through the intervening hours she had danced his brain into a frenzy, yet now, standing before him in the half-light, she seemed to hesitate. Kit too stood motionless, holding his breath in the silence. Dew-kissed curls framed an oval, finely modelled face from which dark eyes searched his. Questioning. And found the selfsame question reflected there. Then Mary smiled. It was as if the sun had suddenly come out. And then she laughed. The light, thin laughter of a fairy child. Kit stared at that luscious mouth, full-lipped, little white teeth parted to reveal the soft, pink tongue. His arms encircled her, his own mouth searching hers hungrily, his tongue tasting and delighting in her sweetness as his hands explored the waistline of her gown for the ties.

A groan forced its way from his throat as Mary pressed herself against him. He could feel every part of her body caressing his through the thin cloth. Impatience made him clumsy as she clung to him and she pulled away, still laughing.

'Your cloak.'

Kit couldn't bring himself to speak as

between them they laid it on the ground, and as Mary promptly sat down on the fine russet wool her garments magically parted company. There was no need for words. His fingers trembled as they finished the job hers had begun and his eyes widened as the hidden treasures were revealed slowly, little by little. His dreams had not prepared him for this perfection. Naked as the day she was born, Mary stretched herself with carefully calculated feline grace. Kit could hold back no longer. He had to touch. Endless silken skin, silver-lustred in the pearl-grey light. Two firm, tip-tilted breasts, dark-nippled, claimed his mouth in turn. Long-limbed as a young colt she lay quiescent as he discovered all her secret places; as he gently probed, inquisitive yet awed, the moistened portal which, to Kit Hatton, still dwelt in the realms of fantasy. Hallowed ground. Virgin ground. The mystery and essence of woman.

His privacy too was being invaded as her expert hands made short work of his points and hose. Had his mind been clearer he would have wondered at her dexterity and the ease with which she aroused his youthful passions to the point of no return. And then he was above her; being guided; being enveloped. The unexpected warmth left him gasping; the supple movements of her flat belly and the soft, rhythmic pressure of her thighs made him moan with ecstasy.

'Mary. Oh, Mary. I don't want to hurt you but . . . Oh . . .'

She had thrust herself against him, taking him deeper than he would have believed possible, and then held him there. Motionless. There was nothing he could do. The whole world throbbed and pulsated with a wild intoxication. Last night, that frenzied dance had hinted at this. He had felt it, little realizing how her movements then had been the merest suggestion. Persuading him to join her in her pleasure. To blend with her. Completely. Kit kissed the now familiar mouth lovingly, reviving echoes of passion as he did so.

In the distance a cock began to crow and Christopher Hatton knew exactly how he felt. The world was a wonderful place. And as if to prove it the sun burst over the horizon, touching the rest of Coneybury Hill.

'How old are you, Mary Shea?'

'Guess. Can you?' Though they were dressed again they still lay on the now ruffled cloak, her hands still caressing; his arm around her shoulders and his hand upon her breast.

'You act older than you look, Are you still a child, or a grown woman? I have no way of knowing.'

'I am a child-woman. A half-grown spirit of the woods and meadows. An imp. An elf. A goblin.'

'Not you.' Kit kissed the end of her nose. 'A fairy queen. An angel who has made the

Squire of Holdenby into a man.'

Mary shook her dark hair and cheekily licked her lips. 'You were no boy. I've never seen a boy so well grown as that!' She tweeked at his hose playfully. 'Nor any man so wholesome.'

'Don't.' Kit turned her face to his, his finger under her chin. 'Don't make it sound so . . . How old are you?'

'Fifteen, sir.' Suddenly Mary's expression was all innocence. If that was how he wanted her, then that was how she would be. He could have anything he wanted of her. Mary Shea recognized good fortune when it smiled and she wasn't one to let it slip through her fingers without a struggle. Mister Hatton was the most handsome young man to cross her path for many a day. Master of Holdenby too! He should be good for a meal or two. Maybe even a gown. Or shoes! What wouldn't she do for a pair of shoes?

Fifteen. A year younger than himself. And so exciting that he was sure he could never let her go. They would be together for ever.

'You will come again tomorrow? You do want to?' Would she want to? Had it been the same for her? It must have been.

'Not here. Somewhere else. Mmm. Tomorrow.' She turned her head to kiss his neck knowing full well that it would make him shiver.

'Anywhere. Mary. My Mary.' The kisses

were endless. 'But why not here? What is wrong with Coneybury Hill all of a sudden?'

'I don't know. It's hard to explain. Put your ear to the ground. Listen. Can you hear anything?'

Kit listened. He shook his head.

Mary's face wore a solemn expression. 'Sometimes I know things. Strange things. And this morning I thought I heard voices. Whispering. From under the ground. Dead voices. Calling me.'

She shuddered and Kit held her tighter.

'You're cold.' He rubbed her arm to warm her.

'No. Not cold. It's just that . . .' She stopped. 'Let's go. I'll meet you tomorrow. Somewhere else.'

That summer the tomorrows seemed to go on forever. And the meeting-places were as varied as the fun they shared together. In Butt's Meadow and Marston's Meadow, and in Ram Meadow where Mary teased that the very name must have inspired him. And in the shelter of the trees. Haily Wood, Crow's Spinney and Middle Close all stood witness to their frolics as Kit sampled pleasures he had previously never even dreamed of; as Mary taught him all she knew, and more besides.

'Close your eyes. I have something for you.'

'Another gift?' Mary was girlish in her excitement, running to him and flinging her arms round his neck. 'Oh, I love you, I love you, my Knight, my Prince, my King.'

'Close your eyes.' Each word was emphasized separately as he tried to remain solemn. It was an impossibility and he was soon grinning at her obvious delight. Kit was now in debt to yet another merchant in the town of Northampton, but that was the furthest thought from his mind at that moment. 'Hold out your hands.'

Mary Shea did so as she screwed her eyes tightly shut. Carefully Kit placed the red kid-leather shoes on the upturned palms.

'Now look.'

Mary stared at the shoes in silence and for a second he thought something was wrong, but as she lifted her face to his he saw with compassion that her lovely eyes were brimming with tears.

'Mary, my love, don't cry.' He held her tight against him and kissed her hair. 'Not for a paltry pair of shoes. If the whole world were mine I would give it to you willingly. You do like them, then?'

For an answer the black-haired tinker's daughter pulled his mouth down onto hers and kissed him as she had never kissed him before.

'You don't understand, do you?' Mary gazed helplessly into the deep sincerity of his sapphire eyes. She ran her fingers through the thick brown hair before bringing them down to stroke the little curls at the nape of his neck. 'There is no need. No need for costly gifts. I love you. And I would still love you if you were a pauper. Oh, it's no use. You don't understand.'

And truth to tell, neither did she. It had started as a game which she had played many times before, though never so successfully, and ended with her wanting to give so much more than her body. But there was nothing else to give. She had nothing else. Or so she had thought. Mary Shea had been brought up to look after herself and had never been squeamish about what sometimes had to be done. But this time it was different. And Kit Hatton didn't understand.

'Of course you love me. Do you think I don't know? After the things we have done? The things you have shown me? Shall I ever forget, though I live to be a hundred, who it was first taught me to dance? Before we met I was more at home on a horse than in the company of ladies, yet not only can I now perform the prim steps of societies' entertainments, but vastly improve upon them too. And the way you have loved me! In sun and summer rain; at dawn and noon and dusk. Soft as moonlight; bright as fireflies; hot as flarne.' He was undressing her, his hands underlining the passion of his words. Mary's hand fluttered briefly, protectively, across her own belly before she too responded to the needs of her body. Of her love.

It wasn't until late August that reality rudely

interrupted Christopher Hatton's not so innocent pleasures. For weeks he had somehow endured the taunts and jibes of the others as they remarked on the shadows under his eyes and his seeming lack of energy at the butts and in the tilt yard. He had shrugged aside their envy with the contempt which it deserved. Until yesterday. Simon Fletcher's crude remarks had been more than mere slight. And directed not at Kit, but at Mary. That was too much and in the space of ten minutes Mister Hatton had proved that his strength had not been sapped enough to render him helpless in a fight. Simon's cries for mercy had been ignored and he had finally escaped, spitting teeth and blood and with a nose which would remain twisted for the rest of his life.

Despite the energetic venting of his spleen, Fletcher's words continued to haunt him. He was wrong! Mary was no whore. Mary was everything a woman should be. Everything? Kit tried not to examine that statement too closely, but it wouldn't be ignored. He knew. Why had he never stopped to think? His uncle, William Saunders, would have an apoplectic fit if the word marriage was even so much as whispered in connection with Mary Shea. Not that Mary had ever hinted at such a thing. She wouldn't. But he had always thought . . . What had he thought? He hadn't, and that was the trouble. He had never thought further than the next day. He had thought that autumn would never come.

It was evening before he tethered his horse at the edge of Thistley Spinney and made his way to the thicket, well away from the lane and the paths of casual travellers. Mary was waiting. She must have heard him approaching, but today there was no warm welcome. She didn't even raise her head to look at him. Had she read his mind? Dropping to his knee and placing his hands on her shoulders he turned her to face him.

'What's wrong?'

Still she wouldn't look.

'Mary. Love? What is it?'

At last the young girl moved. Only as she shook back the tangle of curls from her face did he realize that she was hurt. The dark-red bruise ran from temple to chin and her left eye was swollen and black. A gash puckered her lower lip which began to quiver as the tears began again.

'God's wounds! Who did it? I'll tear him limb from limb!'

Mary shook her head as she sobbed hopelessly. 'No. You can't. It's all my fault anyway.' She sniffed and wiped her nose on her arm. 'I couldn't do it. I couldn't.' She held up the wilted bunch of herbs which had grown warm and withered in her hands during the hours she had cried over them.

'Couldn't do it?' Kit was genuinely puzzled.

'Couldn't do what?'

'Oh Kit.'

She was looking at him as though he was a child. A five-year-old who had committed a mortal sin in all innocence. Gently she took hold of his hand and laid it, palm down, on her belly.

'No longer flat, Kit.'

A child? Did she mean . . .? His child . . .?

'I couldn't.' Mary threw the ragged leaves from her vehemently. 'I thought . . . I wanted to give you something . . . Something special. And then my father threatened to kill me if I didn't get rid of it . . . but I couldn't. I couldn't kill your child. I want your child more than I have ever wanted anything in my life.' Somehow she managed a smile. 'More than I wanted a pair of shoes.'

Kit looked dazed. It was all happening too quickly. Was it only last night that he had realized that there could be no future for them? And now this. Mary, his carefree spirit, nymph of wood and meadow, had been trapped by Mother Nature herself. She loved him, and she couldn't kill his child. And neither could he. No matter what his uncle said he would marry Mary Shea, and in time he would teach her to be a lady. For the first time since he had met her, Kit felt older than Mary. He would look after her. He would protect her. He loved her. Didn't he?

* * *

William Saunders had at first taken it all in good part. What young man didn't have his idle fancies? Better to get your bastards on girls of no account than on girls whose families could ruin you, both socially and politically. No one counted any number of such . . . er . . . occurrences as a bar to a respectable marriage. When the time came. When the right match came along. When, however, his ridiculous young nephew had set forth his outrageous plan to make an honest woman of the tinker's girl it had become quite a different matter.

'Ridiculous! Absolutely out of the question! Your poor father will be turning in his grave to hear his son ranting like a lunatic over some unwholesome peasant, and as for your mother, my poor sister . . . What did she ever do to deserve such an ingrate for a son? Will you dishonour your family name? And mine? For make no mistake about it, your actions will reflect on us all. Your sister too. And your brother Thomas. Ah, how I rue the day the Lord saw fit to take dear Francis from us. Now there was a young man who knew his position in life and strove to uphold it!'

'But, sir . . .'

'No.' Mister Saunders interrupted him sternly. 'No buts! I should have sent you away before this. I see that now, but I could find no harm in the sporting activities you seemed to enjoy. No. You are well overdue some stricter education and I shall be making arrangements for your immediate removal to Oxford. I would recommend that you make the most of your opportunities in that great place of learning. And forget all this nonsense!'

'But . . .' Stubbornly Kit tried to argue.

'Sir, I shall lose patience with you!' A warning flush of anger began to redden William Saunders's jowls. Kit bit his lip in a supreme effort to remain silent. He was getting nowhere, he knew. But he wouldn't abandon Mary. Or his child. Not completely anyway.

William Saunders sighed. The lad was too soft. He'd never amount to much unless he altered his ideas, if not his ways.

'Pay her off then, if you must. If her family will give her no truckle. But make no mistake, this is the last I want to hear on the matter.' So far as Mister Saunders was concerned, the case was closed.

* * *

Inside the Talbot Tavern, bordering the market square in the town of Northampton, Kit Hatton took another long drink of the sweetish ale before stretching his arm about Thomas's shoulders and leaning against him companionably. Here, amidst the general hubbub of the regular clientèle, the world did not seem such a bad place after all. Especially with a belly full of ale. Heated discussions, some almost amounting to arguments, ebbed and flowed round them, woodsmoke from the fire making it difficult in the gloom to identify individuals, and occasionally loud bellows of laughter would sound from some darkened corner to prove that not everything was doom-laden. No doubt the ale-wife, her magnificent paps unlaced and sweat-shined, had a lot to do with the jollity. Most of the serious talk centred on the war with France. It would never do to speak openly against the Queen but it was a well-known fact that her husband, King Phillip of Spain, was not the most popular man in the kingdom. Persuading Queen Mary into a war and then disappearing back to his own realms within weeks! Some thought the French deserved all that was coming to them, but others had more of an eye for their own prosperity and worried that the local crops and husbandry would only lose by it. How could you till and farm with no workers? There were accidents enough without wars. What about that fellow over at Haddon way?

'Mauled by wild beasts, so I heard.'

'Bled to death, certainly, but no wild beast was the culprit. Caught in one of his own traps, he was. Not found until he was completely empty. Flat as a pancake, they say.'

'Poacher, was he? Not a good one or he'd have taken more care not to get caught!'

The men all chuckled into their drinks. There wasn't a one of them who hadn't tried his hand at the same game at some time or other. But that one had been a foreigner anyway. A tinker, they said.

Kit Hatton called for another drink and his friends watched him down it with amused grins. Tomorrow he'd be gone. To Oxford, and a new life.

'It's been a long, hot summer.' John Messinger winked at Henry Dalton. 'Different than usual. Don't you think?'

Christopher Hatton smiled at him drunkenly. 'Different? You don't know the half of it. Have you ever lain naked in the moonlight with an angel? Have you ever swived to exhaustion with a temptress in the noon-day heat? Have you loved until your heart felt that it would burst?'

'No. No, never. Tell us. Tell us what it's like.'

There was a lot of nudging going on but they knew they were safe. Kit was busy re-living his dream.

'So much soft skin. You can call me a liar, but I swear it went on for ever. And when she wrapped herself around me . . .' His eyes had become glazed at the memory. 'Paps . . .' He cupped his hands. 'Just so big . . . and . . .' He licked his lips.

Kit was beginning to slide forward across the table.

'And . . .?' He was prompted.

'And it was unbelievable . . . So many different ways . . . And the little sickle-shaped scar on her arm . . .' He sounded almost asleep.

'And the small brown mole at the base of her spine!'

Simon Fletcher winced as he said the words. John Messinger's boot had a sharp edge to it, and a warning look seemed to ask if he wanted a broken jaw to match his nose. But there was no harm done. Mister Hatton could no longer add two and two together to get any answer whatsoever.

'Dorothy will take care of her. I can trust Dorothy. And you will take care of Holdenby for me, won't you, Tom? Till I come home?'

'Lucky for Mary that your sister is so amenable. What with her father having the accident . . .' In his cups, Simon Fletcher simply couldn't keep his mouth shut.

A bright, vermilion image slashed across Kit's memory and before any of his party could move, or even begin to realize the startling effect which thought sometimes exerted upon the stomach, their friend heaved and sprayed them all with vomit. Such incidents serve to separate the men from the boys and on this occasion it was left to the kind offices of Kit Hatton's neighbour, John Spencer, to see the youngsters safely home.

* * *

Despite the seasonal hindrance of driving rain and sleet, John Messinger covered the fifty or so miles between Northampton and Oxford in record time. Finding Christopher Hatton in that unfamiliar maze was another matter altogether. Wearily he trudged from lodging-house to lodging-house until he almost gave up hope. It was chance which turned his feet towards the door of the inn. That and the cold. And the hunger under his ribs. It was certainly chance which found him standing in Cornmarket at the moment when he decided not to search any more until the morning. He hadn't even removed his cloak, running rivulets across the square stones of the floor, when he heard that familiar laugh ring out above the rest. Stretched comfortably before the hearth, surrounded by others who looked to be at least of equal station, was Mister Hatton. And very elegant he was too in a velvet doublet which must have cost a fortune. The talk was all of plays and theatres and high-sounding literature which was as familiar to John Messinger, the coachman's son, as the Greek alphabet. And as comprehensible. Kit Hatton had changed. Or had he? He was only doing the things required of young men in his position. Landowners. Lords of the Manor. Perhaps it was John who at that moment saw his friend as he really was. Not the wrestling partner, or the adversary at the tilt. Not the young fool who had once fancied himself in love with the tinker's daughter either. Now it was John who felt the fool. And an inferior fool at that! Why on earth had he come? What had made him think Kit would still be interested. The summer was long gone. The best thing to do was leave.

'John! John Messinger! What brings you so far from home in this inclement weather? Come to the fire, sir. Make way, you lazy dogs and pour the man a goblet of hot, spiced wine. Show some hospitality can't you.'

His fellow students, with their quaint and hostile sense of fun, made it a game, bowing and scraping to the newcomer with the most extravagant servility until he was red in the face from embarrassment and wished the floor would open and swallow him.

'Fools. Idiots. Let the man be.'

'Show hospitality! Let the man be! Make up your mind, your Pompousness. Which is it to be?' The thin, red-headed youth strode to and fro as though perplexed by the confusing orders.

It was like a stage show. And badly acted. Overacted! And John stood in the midst of it all, looking lost, and dripping wet.

'John, allow me to introduce my friends. Robert Wilmot, temporary keeper of the wine. That office changes nightly, I might add, as none of us are trustworthy when it comes to keeping wine. Roger Stafford. Imbecile and genius, but mostly, aspiring playwright. And the gentleman helping you off with your cloak is Henry. Henry Noel. A man whose sartorial elegance is equalled only by my own.'

Having removed the cloak, Henry was making a critical assessment of the damp stranger. What he saw did not impress him.

'I think perhaps we should leave Mister Hatton to entertain his guest.'

The others seemed quite happy at that suggestion.

'Bring the wine.'

The three self-opinionated men left John Messinger gasping. Kit Hatton laughed.

'Don't mind them. It is sometimes difficult to tell when they are acting and when they are not but they mean no harm by it. We all aspire to fame and fortune. One way or another. And a pursuit of the arts is seen as an essential part of achieving that ambition. It is a door into Society, that's all. But you haven't come riding through these foul storms simply to pass the time of day. What is it?'

John hesitated. It had seemed so important when he heard and he had been sure that Kit would want to know. But that had been before he met Kit's new friends. Before he had met the new Kit.

'It's Mary Shea.' John waited to see if there was any reaction to that name.

'Mary? What of her?'

The elegant mask vanished and John saw with relief that there was real concern in the cornflower-blue eyes which, he noticed, were exactly matched for colour by the stylish doublet. Kit grasped his arm tightly and John immediately knew that the changes were only superficial. Dancing and poetry had not kept Kit from fencing or the tilt. His sword arm was still too strong for his friend to want to argue with.

'She had a daughter. Yesterday.'

'But . . . She can't have. Not until next month. What did Dorothy say?' Had Simon Fletcher been right after all? Had he been taken for a fool?

'I only heard it from Anne Smallwood who works up at the house now and she said that the child was early. It was a bad birth. Arse about face, as is the way in such cases.' John saw the doubts his news had caused. 'Anne said that Mistress Dorothy believes the child to be four weeks early and at first feared that it would not survive.'

'But it will?' Kit asked anxiously. He wanted it to be his. And he wanted it to live. After all Mary had suffered, it had to live.

'Oh yes. The child will live.' John lapsed into silence and it was several seconds before Kit realized the implications of that silence.

'And Mary? Tell me.'

Still John didn't speak.

'Is she dead? For God's sake, John, tell me.'

John shook his head. 'Not yet. I'm sorry Kit. It's just that I thought you would want to know. I didn't realize . . . all this . . .' He indicated the others who were now performing for other friends on the far side of the room.

'Don't worry. I doubt that Oxford will ever make a gentleman out of me. My heart will always dwell at Holdenby and Holdenby dwells constantly in my heart. You did right to come and tomorrow we shall make the journey home together. Mister Saunders cannot deny me the right to see my child. And my poor Mary.'

* * *

Dorothy Newport watched the tears pour unashamedly down her brother's cheeks as he held the tiny scrap of life in his arms for the first time. Poor Kit! He tried so hard to be what was expected of him, and to any casual observer, he succeeded. But he was barely seventeen and inside his breast beat a tender heart of pure gold which the fates seemed to delight in bruising at every opportunity.

'Meriel. My baby.' He kissed the tiny face, very gently. 'Did she say anything . . . before . . .'

Dorothy felt herself near to tears as she watched his naked suffering. She nodded.

'Tell him to come to me. Some day. Tell him to listen for my voice in the grass as the sunrise touches the crest of Coneybury Hill. I shall be waiting there.'

'Some day.' Christopher Hatton gazed out of the window at the storm-tossed landscape. 'Some day the sun will rise again for me. And then I shall go to her.'

CHAPTER TWO

All the well-chosen words, the wit and humour, and the usual profuse thanks of the speaker were completely lost on Christopher Hatton. Was there anything he had forgotten? Was everyone in their place? First-night nerves were turning his belly into a bag of writhing worms and his bowels to water, and this was not the time to be taken short! Envy demoralized him further as he watched the tall, handsome figure on the dais holding the attention of the whole assembly with ease. But that man was not only tall and handsome. He was also the master of strategy, diplomacy and cunning; a man whose family history was steeped in subterfuge and intrigue, but whose personal charm and intelligence had raised him out of danger. Robert Dudley, Master of the Queen's Horse, brought his oratory to a close and sat down to tumultuous applause. Through his powerful aid the Inner Temple had successfully resisted the transfer of one of their Inns to a rival society and had demonstrated their gratitude by enrolling the Queen's favourite courtier as a Member of the House.

It was time for the Revels proper to begin and Mister Dudley was ready to hold Court. Kit Hatton, desperately swallowing his nervousness, stepped forward to perform his duties as Master of the Game, Henry Noel, his Chief Ranger, at his side, and despite strict rules being laid down as to the manner, cut and colour of the clothes of these two officers, the pair had somehow conceived their uniforms as the height of fashion. The Master of the Game cut a dashing figure in fine green velvet with white silk hose. Tall and handsome, he was a shining example for all young men with athletic aspirations to follow. At the age of twenty-one he was unbeatable in the field. Archery, swordsmanship, or horsemanship. There was none better. And it was the same with the gentler pastimes. Acting seemed to be second nature to him, and in the dance he was an innovator, making new dances out of old. It would have been easy to dislike him. If he hadn't been so charming and personable a fellow!

Having approached the Lord Chancellor and kneeling, declaring his part and that of his companion, the two circled the great Hall of the Inner Temple in opposite directions and on coming together in the centre blew loudly on horns which they carried around their necks. Three great blasts. The signal had been given. At the sound of answering hunting horns the doors were flung open to admit the huntsmen and their hounds, carrying before them a fox and a cat, both these wretched animals being trussed at the end of staves. The Master of the Game then directed that the Ranger of the Forest secured them by their necks to a central stake, and the hounds were released. The pack made short work of it and all new Members were solemnly and ceremoniously bloodied. The feasting could begin!

They were days of gluttony. The main meal of the day began before noon and finished after dark with so many meats and fowl and pies and pastries that they gave up counting. Even supposing that they could have counted after the ale they consumed. Their tongues took on the texture of well-worn leather and blood-shot eyes told their own tale of heads which almost craved the block to cure them of the ache.

Thomas Sackville urged them to drink water.

'This is a serious play and one which has taken me much time and effort to construct. Do you all know your lines? Your postures? Your cues?' He was convinced that the whole thing was going to end in chaos, the more so as he had written the lines in a very different metre from that which the players were used to. Would it work? That was the question Thomas was worrying about. And in addition to the mechanics of the thing, there was the content. Where the succession of the Crown is uncertain, the result is civil war. That was the message spelt out in the tragedy of King Gorboduc and his sons, Ferrex and Porrex. Still, it was no more than the Councillors were saying to Her Majesty's face daily. If his cousin Queen Elizabeth did not marry soon it would be the worse for all of them. Oh, yes. The theme was topical and with luck his efforts would be well received. By some, at any rate.

'You fret like a mother over her pukey babe. And for no good reason. Would we act in a play which was about to fail? Would we have bothered all these weeks to spend our free time learning rubbish? Are you *trying* to insult us?' Henry Noel's freckled face beamed up at Thomas, his goblet still held ostentatiously as though in a toast. 'Believe me Mister Sackville, THE PLAY IS GOOD!'

His companions rose to the occasion, applauding loudly with a variety of affirmatives, stamping their feet and banging on the tables with their empty flagons. Word had most definitely gone before. The play is good!

And so it proved when finally played to perfection, everyone knowing their parts. The members of that élite, the Inner Temple, praised it to the skies. Never in the history of

England had any other Society trodden new ground so well and to such effect. Anyone with half an eye, they said, could see that from this day on, playwrights must look to their laurels. Blank verse like that of Thomas Sackville would be the only medium for the future. From today, all other scribbling was rendered obsolete.

* * *

Grinning to himself in the semi-darkness, Kit Hatton strolled slowly back along the corridors of Whitehall towards the great hall, savouring the excitement and adulation of the audience which had been his only a bare half-hour before. He could scarcely believe his luck. To have played before the Queen! It was an honour he had never looked for but one which he would cherish for a lifetime, he was certain. She had watched him with such measured concentration. So much understanding that it was unnerving. An intelligent woman, too intelligent for a woman some had said, she could not have failed to read the message woven into the plot. And yet she *had* enjoyed it. What's more, she had noticed him. Of that Kit Hatton was sure. As with any actor, he could sense when he was watched personally and not just in the part cast for him. Fame and fortune! Ah, how they had dreamed their dreams and righted the world over their cups.

How they were convinced that they were right and the whole world was just too blind to see it. And now the Queen had looked at him! He hadn't felt like this since Mary . . .

Ahead of him a door opened and closed in the dim light. Someone else was making their way to the hall for the dancing. A rustle of skirts. A woman. No . . . a girl. No more than fourteen or fifteen years old. As she moved beneath the flickering light of a torch held high in its sconce on the wall he saw briefly the black curls bounce and tremble; the hips twitch in a way he had almost forgotten. The spring in her step. The very joy of living.

'Mary! Mary, is it you?' The words had escaped before he realized he had spoken.

'Yes?' She stopped and turned, her face hidden by shadows. 'Who is it? Do I know you, sir?'

'Mary. My Mary.' Without even being conscious of approaching her he found himself taking the girl in his arms and kissing her.

'Sir! I beg you! Are you drunk? Leave or I shall scream for the guard. Her Majesty will have you flogged for this. She is most particular about the conduct of her ladies. Leave I say!'

She had no need to continue. Kit stood gazing down at her, stammering like a schoolboy. Trying to apologize. To explain. His mind had been on other things . . . On things long past . . . He had thought that she was . . .

'I'm sorry. I mistook you for a friend I once knew. Her name was Mary.' He could see now he was close that the resemblance was only superficial. This girl was a lady of the Court, refined and genteel, and oh so haughty in her manners. Mary Shea would never have looked at a man like that, no matter what his business.

'As is mine, and for that reason only did I halt when you called. I can assure you that I am not in the habit of keeping assignations in darkened hallways with strangers.' Her little nose went up in the air as she tried to look down on him, which was quite impossible as he towered over her slight figure.

'That, Mistress, I can quite believe,' he answered dryly, 'And if you will permit me I shall pay for my mistake by escorting you back to the protection of the crowds.'

With a barely perceptible nod of her head the young woman accepted the offer and as he took her arm Kit Hatton felt a thrill run through him which he thought he had lost for ever. First his best-ever performance, and now this! All in a single night. There must be magic in the air. And still the dance to come! When she danced with him her reserve would thaw and he could make her better acquaintance. He knew, without vanity, that there were very few men as handsome present, and none so adept on the floor. He had come a long way from 'The Hay,' 'Tom Tyler' and 'John Come Kiss Me,' and all the other country prancings of his youth in Holdenby. Stately as any in the pavane, he had improved the simple steps of the cinquepace into a galliard so intricate and nimble that he knew all eyes would be on him as he trod the measure. Being expert with the sword did not prevent him from cutting a fine caper too! Then perhaps this little black-haired, blacked-eyed beauty would smile at him.

She didn't. Oh, she danced with him, but so disdainfully that it almost looked as though she thought him no better than a peasant; as though he had trodden in something foul and forgotten to wipe his shoe. As though she found him repulsive in the extreme! Kit's bubble of euphoria burst and by the time he had returned her to her place amongst the Queen's ladies he felt completely deflated.

How? How could one young woman whose name he didn't even know do this to him? His friends didn't help matters, having watched his vain attempts to attract the girl's interest, in itself a novelty, they couldn't help but indulge in playful ridicule.

'Perhaps she needs more than a fine leg to tempt her, eh? But what? A gift? Some can be bought.' Bartholomew Tate was Kit's cousin, their mothers being sisters, and he knew more than most the thread-bare state of Mister Hatton's pockets.

'No! Poetry. Try sweet words in her ear. They are cheaper and leave no evidence should she try to trap you at a later date.' Roger Stafford was at present trying to extricate himself from such an encounter, the young woman concerned attempting to make a permanent bond by waving the jewel he had beggared himself buying in his face.

'Carry her off and bed her and she'll soon come to your way of thinking.' With the applause still ringing in his ears, Henry Noel could believe anything possible tonight.

'And land myself in the Tower? If you care to use your eyes you will see that she is in the Queen's retinue, and you well know Her Majesty's views on moral laxity.' Christopher Hatton shook his head despondently. 'I don't even know her name, except that she answered when I called her Mary, thinking her to be someone I knew.'

'Forget her then. There are plenty of others more willing.' Mister Noel would not let anything interfere with pleasure tonight.

Kit Hatton allowed himself a rueful smile. 'But isn't it always the way. There is no other woman in this room worth a second glance. Not one!'

'Begging your pardon, sir, I have been asked by Lord Robert to bring you into Her Majesty's presence.'

That statement stopped the discussion immediately and Kit found himself gaping rather stupidly at Hawthorne, Lord Robert Dudley's man.

'Better revise your last observation on the female company.' Henry said this in a loud aside, his hand half shielding his mouth as in a play.

'Me? Approach the Queen?' Kit was still convinced that there must be a mistake.

'If you are Mister Christopher Hatton, then I do indeed mean just that. And it would be best if you did not keep her waiting.'

The pressure of the man's hand on his elbow set Kit's feet in motion and his heart banging. What did the Queen want with him? Had the mysterious Mary accused him of rape in the corridor? No. It couldn't be that or she would not have danced with him earlier. What then? As he knelt before Queen Elizabeth he could feel the dark girl's eyes burning into him with something almost akin to hate. Yet why should she hate him? They had never met until this night and she could know nothing of him. The Queen bade him rise and sit beside her, and for the moment the questions must remain unanswered.

'Your Majesty, this is Mister Christopher Hatton, Member of the Inner Temple and a most able student of the Arts as borne out by his admirable performance tonight and his fastidious execution of the part of Master of the Game at the Christmas Revels.' Robert Dudley made the introduction.

'I congratulate you, sir. You come highly recommended by Lord Roberts.' The Queen tapped the hand of her favourite courtier happily. 'And I should like to hear a little about your life from your own lips. If you feel so disposed.'

'Your Majesty does me great honour and I am reduced to a trembling wreck in the presence of one whose whole being radiates beauty and grace. My life has been dull and insignificant until this very moment and there is nothing to tell.'

The Queen did learn, however, of his holdings in Northamptonshire, and of his education at Oxford.

'So now you are to take a degree in Law?' By the disbelieving smile Kit could tell that the Queen was unable to see him as a dusty academic.

'After tonight my heart is no longer in such studies. My heart is lost to the fairest maiden in the land.' Could she hear? Kit kept his eyes on the laughing blue ones of his Queen but surely Mary would realize that the words were meant for her. He wouldn't lose an opportunity to make an impression on Her Majesty if it would bring him into closer proximity to Mary.

'I watched your galliard, sir, and I confess that I have never seen it performed so skilfully or so . . . gracefully.' Whatever the word the Queen had in her mind, she changed it. 'You shall show it to me. I would perform it as you do and perhaps together we can improve on it even further.'

The Court stared goggle-eyed. Queen Elizabeth, slender as a wand and supple as a blade of grass, with a mass of red-gold hair, shimmering with every twist and turn and caper; and Christopher Hatton, tall and beautifully proportioned in limb and body. The handsome youth had a superbly controlled strength. Elegance without arrogance. A style which set female bellies quivering, bitches on heat every one of them, and a disarming quality which made him so approachable. So human. Except, of course, for the fact that it was the Queen who held his hand. And she seemed disposed to go on holding it, for the rest of that night, at least. Elizabeth had found herself another favourite!

Mary Fytton watched the whole performance dispassionately.

'I think you've found yourself another admirer.' Meg Clifford whispered in her ear. 'And if I hadn't already been more than satisfied with my own bedmate, I would be envious.'

'No need to be,' her companion retorted. 'He'll get no more encouragement than the rest. Single-minded animals, the lot of them!'

Meg shrugged her shoulders. There was something very odd about a young woman of Mary's age and positive good looks dismissing every suitor out of hand. It wasn't just that the Queen actively discouraged promiscuity amongst her ladies. In this case, it was more than that, but what, she didn't know. She had known Mary since the day she arrived at Court with her nurse, Meg's old friend Elizabeth Fytton. A woman who knew more about the mysteries of the herb-garden than anyone on earth. Meg had learnt a lot from Mistress Fytton, and even now, when time permitted, she would journey across to Wiltshire to increase her knowledge of potions and cures. And other remedies best not spoken of! But Mary was a mystery in herself. No one really knew who she was, or why Elizabeth Tudor kept her so close. And the Queen had made it quite clear that she did not want the subject discussed. Whoever she was, the girl had a high opinion of herself which kept many of the women distant and the only person she would confide in was Meg. And in that confidence she was sparing. Look at her now, watching Lord Robert through the corner of her eye, thinking herself unobserved. She was a strange one! No-one in their right minds would set their cap at Robert Dudley. Especially one so close to the Queen. If Her Majesty ever suspected . . .

Mary Fytton found herself drawn to Robert against all her natural instincts. He fascinated her. Fascinated her because he and the Queen . . . Had they? Had they ever made love during those long, long hours they had been alone together in the Queen's private chambers?

Unconsciously, Mary clenched her fists as her stomach seemed to twist itself into knots. Jealousy was a painful emotion. The thought of him touching Elizabeth's beautiful white skin . . . The thought of Elizabeth running her fingers through that thick black hair . . . Kissing. Caressing. What was he thinking as he watched the wanton movements of that temptress as she pranced across the floor, flirting with an anonymous law student? Giving an insignificant subject a single moment of glory which he would remember all his life!

Some sixth sense alerted Robert to her interest in him and he turned towards her enquiringly only to find that Mary averted her gaze immediately. A strange child. Didn't mix with the other women much. Nor men either! Many an earthy young blood had been sent away from that one with his tail between his legs and a flea in his ear. A pity really. She was quite a beauty. But without a smile even the most gorgeous creature on earth didn't merit the effort. And she had no social standing either, except the Queen's patronage. Which brought his mind back to the fellow now holding Elizabeth's attention. He would have to keep a close eye on Mister Hatton, just in case the boy had ideas of ousting, or at least trying to oust, the Queen's favourite courtier.

What had been in his mind as he studied her? Mary would dearly have liked to know.

Did he find her attractive? As attractive as he found the Queen? But was it really Elizabeth he wanted, or her Crown? Was that the true object of his desire? Robert was an ambitious man, but that was one aspect of human nature which the Queen was constantly aware of, as Mary had been made to appreciate from the moment she arrived at Court. And if she was inclined to forget, there was usually some other member of the Court in trouble over that very thing to remind her. Why, even as she stood there thinking about it, wasn't Edward Seymour, Earl of Hertford, kicking his heels in the Tower for supposedly marrying Katherine Grey without the Queen's permission? He must have been very stupid, or very much in love, to risk the Queen's anger as he had done. Edward Seymour. Seymour! Mary tested the word inside her head. Savoured it. Ah, if these brittle courtiers, so free with their condemnation of those they thought lowly, had only known! If Robert Dudley only knew! Would he then dismiss her with a glance? Would his ambition let him? And would she let him . . .? As the Queen had . . . .? Could she bear that exquisite pain? Welcome his brutal depravity? Indulge his every whim to mortify her flesh; to cleanse her soul? To make her forget the time when, to her humiliation, that other Robert, whilst professing to love her, had stood and gaped as . . . as . . .! Mary shuddered. May the Devil catch up with him, wherever he tried to hide!

*   *   *

Far from the icy blasts of an English winter, Robert Winchcombe was startled to feel the warmth of the still supple flesh. Smooth, ebony flesh, glistening in the sharp azure and gold of an endless Caribbean day. And dead. She had breathed her last aboard a trading ship, robbing them of their bounty. Yet despite her, the slave ship would one day return home safe to harbour laden with precious cargoes of spice and Spanish gold. Lifeless flesh couldn't grow cold in the piercing heat of these tropical waters, and Robert had lately grown familiar with the disgusting results of leaving carcasses lying around for too long. The nauseous stink of the living cargo below decks was bad enough, though he knew it was something he would eventually get used to, but when a corpse was undiscovered, bloated and festering hour after hour, it was more than his stomach could take. Rotten entrails spilling in shiny profusion from a burst belly were not to be contemplated too often. No. She would have to go over the side. And quickly.

Something made him hesitate. The girl was no more than twelve or thirteen years old, though the proud tilt of nipples on newly swelling breasts and the tightening roundness of her abdomen told their own tale of men's baser lusts. She was the last female on board. Not that it would make much difference to many of the crew. There were still plenty of boys below the decks. Robert sat back on his haunches, leaning his head and shoulders carefully against the blistering timbers of the ship as he closed his eyes. Damn the salt-spray! How it stung! If anyone were to notice they would accuse him of crying. But why couldn't he forget? Even the harsh realities of his chosen lifestyle couldn't blot out the horror of his cowardice.

The gentle rocking motion combined with the regular creaking of the vessel to soothe his pain, like the cradle in which his mother had once rocked him softly to sleep. In the kitchen of the manor of Littlecote. The only home he had ever known. Amongst the people he had loved. Seeing day after day the only girl he had ever loved. The gloss of her black hair had been unreal. Moonlight caught in a midnight web. How the twitch of those hips and the tilt of that kissable mouth had tormented him, filling his head with ungentlemanly thoughts. And how those dark eyes had first teased him, and then scorned him, making him ashamed. Then hurt. And then angry. He shouldn't have been angry. It had only clouded his judgement and held him back from . . .

There he was. Making excuses for himself again! Coward! Go on. Admit it. You are nothing but a coward.

Unshed tears had formed themselves into a hard, inflexible ball halfway down his throat, threatening to choke him. He saw again the slim, childish body. Twelve years old. Naked from the shoulders down. Watched the brute strength of Mister Darrel force it face down onto the beaten earth of the old barn floor. Heard again the muffled screams from heaped skirts and petticoats flung up over her head, covering that wealth of shining hair. Rigid with fear he had witnessed the perverted abuse of her innocent flesh. Mister Darrel would have been better served aboard this ship. There were only boys left!

Sea-wind snapped at the sails; a whip-lash sound which jerked his eyes open to the blinding light of the present. The great golden orb blazed down, gilding the mainmast into a sceptre, reminding him of the royal insignia which had cast their long and powerful shadows deep into the heart of the Wiltshire countryside to scurry her away. She had been no ordinary kitchen maid. He was certain of that now. Why else should Mary Fytton be provided with a place at Court? Waiting on the Queen, if rumour was to be believed. As his sister Edith had commented, Queen Elizabeth was not the one to have mere scullery maids waiting on her in her chamber,

The noisy crack of the canvas had done more than bring the boy-sailor out of his past. With surprise and delight he stared unbelievingly as the little negro girl flickered her eyelids open to gaze at him in silent agony. There was no fear in that look. No hate. Just despair. A despair as raw and bloody as her crotch. A despair which had seen death leap out of reach on the devil's breath; the hot winds carrying her ever further from her homeland and into hell. Why had no one warned her?

'Stay away from the lagoons,' they had said. 'Be careful of the swamp. Beware the warriors from the hills.'

Never once had they mentioned the white menace from the sea. Better the crocodiles than this. Better the Ashanti!

Pity nudged briefly at Robert's elbow, but as usual aboard John Hawkins's ship, it found no anchorage. No man with any sense pitied the Christmas goose as its neck was wrung. God's wounds! He had almost thrown her over the side. And she was the last female on board!

'Oi! Land Oi!' Wat Millar's rusty voice rattled through the rigging to those about their business on the decks.

Well. Maybe there would soon be a choice after all. Or maybe there would be other things to think about for the next few weeks. Spaniards, for example. Robert felt excitement pound his blood more fiercely than any slave-girl could. Or any other woman for that matter. Even . . . even the one he was running away from. Hand over sweaty hand he hoisted himself aloft to catch his first glimpse of turquoise spray on white coral sand, edging the jungle of an island. Haiti? Nervous exhilaration overflowed in peals of laughter as he screwed his eyes against the sun. Would they have to fight? His knuckles showed white through the sunburnt skin as he hung easily from the ropes. Now he would prove himself as good a man as any. Coward? Robert Winchcombe was about to show the world what he was really made of!

*   *   *

'Who is she? Where does she come from? Such creamy skin set against that thick, black hair, and a flash of spirit in the eyes which has me itching to tame her.'

'And don't forget those firm young duckies,' Robert Dudley smiled at Kit's enthusiasm. 'Asking to be caressed. I remember when Mary first appeared at Court. Pretty enough, but skinny. No flesh at all in those days. Not worth a second glance.'

'She is now though.' Kit sighed. 'Not from you, I admit.' He raised an eyebrow in the direction of the Queen. Rumours were flying that marriage had recently been mentioned in connection with Lord Robert and Her Majesty.

Robert's answer to that unspoken query was a rather uncertain laugh. He had stayed the best part of several nights in the Queen's own apartments over the festive season and could truthfully say that he had slept with Elizabeth Tudor. She had allowed his kisses and caresses and on one occasion had seemed on the point of capitulation, only to stop him at the last moment. After hours of patient courtship and control, and not a little of her finest wine, he had fallen asleep. Briefly. Just long enough for him to be able to say that he had slept with the Queen of England. And then she had taken a fancy to Christopher Hatton, eight years younger than herself, and Robert had found himself on his guard once more. Despite her reassurances that if she had to marry an Englishman it would be none other than her darling Robin! In that area he was taking no chances but he had soon realized that although Kit was profuse and poetic in his flattery of Elizabeth, his amorous desires lay with one of her younger maids. In that frame of mind he would pose no threat at all.

'Have you any idea where she came from? Hasn't the Queen told you?' Kit was determined to know.

'To be honest, I haven't given the child much thought, but now that you mention it there would seem to be some mystery about her. I remember the day she arrived, brought here by the old woman who could work miracles with ailments. Elizabeth Fytton. If my memory serves me correctly, Mistress Fytton had once been in the household of Queen Katherine Parr, which is where she would first have met our present Queen. What happened to her afterwards I wouldn't know. The child is called Mary Fytton, but whether she is the old woman's kin or not I have no way of knowing. Or why the Queen should so easily be persuaded to take her into her care and protection. I shouldn't ask the Queen if I were you. In many ways her rule is law, and being a woman, it is the small mysteries such as this which often inflame her temper most. Ask the girl herself. That is the best place to get your answer.'

'She won't even speak to me. In fact I have noticed that she rarely speaks at all. To anyone.'

'Meg Clifford, Lady Strange, may be able to help you. When not in attendance they are often together, though what the connection is I don't know. But surely there are warmer bedfellows than that one?' Robert knew that if he himself waited for the Queen in that direction he would have been celebate yet.

'She treats me coldly,' Kit smiled at his own understatement, 'But there is fire in her belly for the right man. I can sense it.'

'And in the meantime?' Now that Robert thought about it it had been a while since he had had a woman himself. And the care one had to take! Not a whisper of such things must reach the Queen's ear. She was a very jealous woman and although she would not satisfy her many admirers herself, woe betide any woman who dared to dream of giving, or even selling favours to one of her puppets. Woe betide the man who dared to look elsewhere for favours!

'In the meantime,' Kit grinned, arousing himself from his dismal thoughts of unrequited desire, 'I shall be away to the Cross Keys where there is always something to take my mind from misery.'

'The Cross Keys?'

'A meeting-place for actors and the like. Good ale. And good food from Jane Penny's kitchen if you will. Good conversation.' Kit paused. 'Have you never seen Jane Penny's daughters?'

Robert shook his head. 'Never even heard of them.'

'That's what comes of aiming high,' Kit chuckled. 'Would you like to see what you are missing.' The glint of mischief in his eyes was unmistakable.

'Mistress Penny's daughters not withstanding, I should like to meet some of your acting friends. This new play of Thomas's has me intrigued and I need some diversion from . . . politics.'

'When you are free, then?' Kit Hatton was pleased. He didn't think that Mister Dudley would be disappointed.

He wasn't. Visibly more relaxed amongst the frivolous, deadly seriousness of the acting fraternity Robert Dudley felt himself being drawn into their wrangles and discussions about their art. Who were the best performers? Who the best writers? The insecurity of the strolling players and the condescension of the gentlemen players! He didn't notice that Kit had slipped away to have a quiet word with the buxom Jane.

Would she mind? For Lord Robert? And not a word! Not a word to anyone that he had been there. Jane Penny was the last one to want the Queen's wrath descending on her establishment. Business was doing very well and she had no need to boast that the Queen's favourite was frequenting the inn.

'You'll pardon us, gentlemen?' Kit bowed with a flourish as he indicated that Robert should follow him through to the private room at the back.

No one so much as raised an eyebrow. The conversation continued as though there had been no interruption. Only Robert looked surprised. More so as he was ushered forward by Mistress Penny herself, her hair now having been scraped and combed into some sort of order, and a grin almost splitting her face in two. She was a plump and obliging figure, not much above thirty years of age, and many a young aspiring actor had found comfort from his troubles in her knowledgeable, all-embracing arms. Those who had the inclination for a woman's arms, that is. There were those who preferred boys taking the female roles, much as they did in their parts on the stage. A door was pushed open and Kit led Robert through. What he found had his mouth falling open like a novice. Mister Hatton made the introductions.

'May I present Mistress Alice Penny, and Mistress Anne Penny.'

Their partly unlaced bodices were cut short below their breasts. Pale and perfect mounds, ornamented by neat, pink nipples, were peeping temptingly through folds of filmy white gauze. Waists so tiny that a man's hand could span them. Pretty, piquant faces crowned by gleaming auburn hair which rippled endlessly down. Mouths, smiling with encouragement, could incite a riot of kisses. And they were identical. Alike as two peas. Or two Pennies!

'Would you like them to serve you with a private supper?' Kit was certain of Robert's answer. 'There is just one thing you should know. They are inseparable. What one does, the other must do. You understand?'

Robert understood very well and laughed indulgently, shaking Kit's hand by way of thanks.

'Till later then.' Christopher Hatton winked broadly as he pulled the door closed behind him.

Friendship without rivalry. That was what Kit had been aiming for in his relationship with Robert Dudley, and that was exactly what he achieved. From now on he could flatter the Queen to the skies without worrying about a knife in the back from her favourite, and continue to show himself to advantage before the beautiful and mysterious Mary Fytton. But things were never straightforward at Elizabeth Tudor's Court, as Kit was soon to find out.

Robert Dudley had his spies everywhere and the fact of Mister Kyle, attaché to the Swedish Embassy, being ready to renew the King of Sweden's suit with Elizabeth was known to him before anyone else got wind of it. What promises were going to be made this time? Elizabeth loved flattery. And gifts. The last thing Robert wanted was for her to be distracted from her promise to him earlier in the year. God's death! Hadn't she as good as told him that she would marry no one but her Robin? There must be no outside interference at this stage. He had as good as won her over. All he needed was a little more time. And that could be bought if only he could get to Kyle before he approached the Queen or Council.

But Robert Kyle was no novice at these games and by a little subterfuge of his own managed to avoid everyone of Lord Robert's men.

'Hell's teeth! What do I pay for? I'll have the man imprisoned on some fine charge or other! Someone must know where he is hiding!' Robert's darkly handsome features were flushed with the impotence of his anger. Lucky for Mister Kyle that he was nowhere to be found at that moment! His life would not have been worth a groat. Kit Hatton made himself scarce. His policy had always been to make friends, not enemies, and at times like these the Cross Keys, or The Boar on East Cheap, seemed more welcoming than usual.

It was as well he had been prudent. The hot July sun was streaming in through the windows of the Presence Chamber as the Queen sat amongst a number of her courtiers and ladies. She was over-gay. Playing a part as only Elizabeth could, though for the moment no one could find cause for any upset. Kit was silent as he stood beside the cushion-strewn window seat watching the bright rays glinting and dancing in Mary's dark hair as she bent her head over her embroidery. She seemed totally unaware of his presence. Completely indifferent to his nearness as he studied her. Why? He might as well be invisible for all the notice Mistress Fytton took of him; as he yearned for her; hungered for her; pined for her. Was her coolness the spur which drove him?

> 'And graven with diamonds in letters plain
> There is written her fair neck about:
> "Noli me tangere, for Caesar's I am,
> And wild for to hold, though I seem tame."'

Kit attempted to gain a smile from her with Tom Wyatt's poetry, that erstwhile lover of Anne Boleyn being long since dead, but still quoted by love-sick swains throughout the land. His reward was a withering look of contempt, heart-felt and indisputable.

'Why, sir, do you persist in wasting your time and ruining my leisure? Will no-one else speak with you either that you have to pester me. What does it take to convince you, sir? I have no liking for you. Nor shall I ever have.'

And with that she turned her attention back to her work, dismissing him with silence, knowing that she had reduced him from a favoured courtier of her mistress the Queen to the insignificant insect he undoubtedly was.

Kit was at a loss to understand her. Did she really find him so repulsive? Common sense told him that she couldn't. Not when so many others were more than willing. Had he wanted them! So what did he have to do to win her? If only he knew!

Then, almost magically, her attitude changed. It was as though she had been waiting, ears pricked and nose twitching, for his footstep outside the door. Suddenly alert and watchful, Mary never took her eyes from Robert Dudley as he strode across to Elizabeth. Kit's heart sank. Was that it? Was it Robert she loved? If so, her love was wasted. Unless she was prepared to lower herself to the level of a passing fancy. Robert was striding confidently towards his mistress. He saw no other woman.

The Queen's brittle laughter faded ominously and a tight silence descended on the chamber. Here was the cause of Elizabeth's unease. A lover's quarrel was about to erupt and those present waited in motionless anticipation. They were not disappointed. The Queen had heard of Robert's interference in the matter of the Swedish ambassador and the young woman, sole ruler of England, would not tolerate such disgraceful behaviour towards any foreign emissary. But it was more than that. It had been a deliberate attempt on Lord Robert's part to interfere with her diplomacy. And that was unforgivable.

'. . . with your spies and gutter-dogs spattering their own filth, trying to make it stick to one whose only crime is to bring me news of an honourable gentleman . . .' She paused for breath. 'A King! No mere commoner hoping to climb to who knows what dizzy heights on the backs of others far more worthy by both birth and nature. What is more, and mark this well, I could never, never for a single moment comtemplate marriage to one who would stoop to such low, immoral behaviour.'

For Kit Hatton this was an inauguration. He had heard of Her Majesty's fearful tongue but witnessing the performance gave the lie to all the tales. It was worse than he had been led to believe. Much worse. Even so, Robert's attitude to his predicament served to show the audience that he shared an intimacy with their monarch boasted by no one else in the land. He did not even try to hide his own anger which flared to match Elizabeth's own.

'Then, Your Majesty, I have no other course open to me but to beg to relieve you of the sight of me. Have I permission to travel overseas?' His tone held a challenge. They were fencing with each other.

'Granted.' The Queen didn't hesitate.

Kit was watching Mary's face during the heated exchange. Did she hope that quarrels like this would further her own cause in the long run? If the Queen cast Robert off for good, then would he look at other women? Perhaps the foolish girl imagined that a simple love-potion from Meg Clifford would turn Robert's thoughts in her direction! Ha! Then she didn't understand the ambitious nature of the man she lusted for! All the airs and graces she so carefully cultivated would be no use whatsoever. A lowly maid would never procure the interest of a Dudley. Ever! So . . . if that really was the way of it . . . Kit began to think he might eventually have a chance with her after all. If he had the patience! If Elizabeth did marry Robert . . . And even if she didn't Mary would realize that she was wasting her time. All Kit had to do was make sure that his arms were the ones she fell into when the time came. Then it would be a short step to the altar, and before she knew what was happening she would be filling the rooms of his dream palace with children.

But just look at her! Poised on the edge of her seat, ready to run to him. To defend him against the Queen's anger!

'You aim too high, Mistress.'

Just for a second she looked shaken. As though he had pierced that impenetrable armour. Then it was gone, her composure regained.

'Sir! There are things in this life which I fear you cannot begin to understand. Nor, I think, would you wish to if given the opportunity. I may not have the experience of age, but I have the benefit of having lived amongst the people of the Court for some years. I warn you to tread warily. Beware of treading on the toes of the mighty lest you find yourself trampled to death. By that I mean leave me alone!' The words were almost a threat.

'Trampled to death? For admiring you?'

'For desiring me.' Repugnance at the very thought came clearly through to him in both her voice and the expression on Mary's face. She turned to watch as Robert Dudley swept out of the room, head held high and anger still showing in every taut sinew of his body. Then he was gone, in a swirl of black and scarlet velvet.

All eyes were on the Queen. Her fine-boned

hands gripped the splendidly carved arms of the chair as she watched his retreating back. Fool! What a stupid fool the man was. Didn't he know her yet? Didn't he know her strength? Her determination? The gods had ordained that she should be Queen of England and no man, not even one she had known and liked all her life, was going to take that from her by becoming her husband, and so, King. Never! Let him kick and shout and stamp his feet! Let others similarly whine and simper. She could play them one against the other and always be the one to win.

Slowly Elizabeth allowed herself to relax into the cushions of her great chair and for a moment she closed her eyes. And yet how close she had come to giving in to female frailty. It was lonely sometimes. Very lonely. And she acknowledged that she was after all only human. But the brutal, physical love of a sweaty, panting male was not the answer, especially when all he saw in her eyes was the glitter of the Crown. Memories of Thomas Seymour still haunted her dreams. His was the first naked flesh to touch hers, and how she had wanted him to take her. Completely. And how he had tried! But he had been married to her father's widow, Queen Katherine Parr, at the time, and Elizabeth herself had been only a foolish young girl who never gave a thought to the fact that one day she might be Queen. It was frightening to think what she might have thrown away by her craving for human affection. It had happened years ago but she could still see that handsome, smiling face, and remember the thrill of love before she had so much to lose. But Thomas was long gone. Opening her eyes, her glance fell on the handsome young couple sitting together on the window seat. Mary. And Christopher Hatton. No! That she would never allow! Jealousy warmed her pale complexion and sharpened her voice.

'Mistress Fytton!' The royal finger beckoned.

Mary laid aside her work and moved to curtsey in front of the Queen. Kit stood to watch her sway gracefully across the herbs and grasses lying thick on the floor, filling the room with the sweet smell of summer. Was she right? Would it mean trouble for her if he persisted in his advances? Certainly the Queen had seen fit to remove her from his company, though that could be mere coincidence, Mary's words making him question the Queen's motives.

'I think it is time that my dress was prepared for my afternoon stroll. You may help Lady Dorothy today and perhaps keep out of mischief.' Lady Dorothy Stafford was Mistress of the Queen's Robe and a stickler for perfection. Elizabeth was granting Mary no favours and they both knew it.

'And in the meantime, I shall tread a

measure or two with my dear Mister Hatton. Have we music?'

If the Queen wished, courtiers would provide it. There were not many of them who were not accomplished at some instrument or other and when Elizabeth spoke, they jumped to do her bidding. As men should. And without demanding the Crown as payment for friendship. Kit took her hand, smiling compliments as he did so and for the first time that day the Queen's own smile held genuine warmth. Let Robin cool his heels a while. He would not go far and would come running the moment she wanted him again. And in the meantime, there were others as handsome and charming. And younger. And they would willingly dance to her tune.

CHAPTER THREE

Bay Speedwell obediently slowed his pace from a canter until he was walking comfortably through the misty dampness of fallen leaves at his master's command. Kit Hatton breathed deeply, tasting winter's first chill in the air as he watched two riders disappear from view into the wraithes of early morning fog. Only the continuing thud of hoofbeats in the distance indicated their direction. He smiled to himself. There was no doubt about it.

Elizabeth was an excellent horsewoman, and he, in company with many others, enjoyed the pleasure of these energetic outings. He also knew just how far to go, and when to leave the field clear to Robert. With the rest of the courtiers and ladies he followed at a safe distance, marking time and making conversation.

'Your brother is still the only one able to keep pace with Her Majesty.' Kit drew alongside Mary Sidney, noticing as he did so that Mary Fytton dropped back a step or two, putting several other ladies between himself and her.

Lady Sidney frowned. 'I don't know that she should be riding out in the damp air this morning. Last night she suffered a blinding headache and I was certain that she was sickening for some illness. I told Robert not to let her ride too far but once they get going there seems to be no stopping them. But perhaps excercise will blow the cobwebs away. She has been wrestling with the problem of the Huguenots, fearing that if Guise is allowed to massacre those people he will turn his Catholic armies against England next.' Mary sighed. 'It is too big a load for a woman to carry alone.' If only her brother Robert could achieve his ambition! That the Queen thought highly of their family was borne out by the fact that she had sent Mary's elder brother, Ambrose, Earl of Warwick, to hold the garrison at Havre. But would she elevate them even further by marrying that charmer Robert? Only time would tell.

Kit knew what she was thinking. 'Somehow I cannot see her as a humble wife with a clutch of infants at her knee. She has too much spirit. Too much fire and leadership, for all that she is a woman.'

'Then as a woman she will never know what she misses.' Mary Sidney's son Philip was now eight years old and her baby daughters, Ambrosia and Mary, were a constant delight to her when she was not called in attendance on the Queen. 'But as a Queen she surely knows the folly of not securing the succession?'

Robert Dudley's son the next true King of England? Mister Hatton marvelled at the aspirations of some families. All he wanted was the smile of a young and comparatively unimportant lady-in-waiting and he couldn't even manage that! He turned in his saddle to watch as she rode beside Henry Darnley. She didn't usually keep company with men. But then Henry was hardly a man! His pretty, girlish face was quite in keeping with his somewhat mincing walk. Why? How could she prefer young Darnley to a real man? Would he ever understand her? Any more than men could understand Elizabeth for not wanting to submit to their desires; for not willingly prostrating herself before the altar of their superiority.

Mary Sidney's fears turned out to be well founded. Some hours after the party had returned to the warmth of Hampton Court the Queen again complained that she felt unwell and asked her ladies to prepare a bath as her skin seemed to prickle with sweat. Mary supervised the operation personally, enlisting the help of Mistress Fytton to dry and perfume the Queen's body after the washing.

Mary Fytton's hands were as gentle as rippling silks as she smoothed the oils and unguents into Elizabeth's white, almost transparent skin. How soft her body felt. Soft yet firm. Feminine yet with a subtle strength which was almost boyish. Slim and straight. Massaging the shoulders and long, elegant neck, trying to relieve the pain of that nagging headache, Mary could feel the Queen's naked vulnerability through her fingertips. Beneath the regal manner and the formal trappings of State, Elizabeth was human. But how human? Despite the pressure being brought to bear from all sides she was still avoiding marriage. Still avoiding childbearing where with most monarchs it was the primary aim in life. To secure the succession. For their own offspring. Why? What made this Queen different? It could be nothing like the childhood nightmare, the sheer brutality which had made masculinity an anathema to Mary. No. Or Lord Robert would not have stayed alone with

Elizabeth in her chambers as he had. For long hours. Even the whole night on occasion! He was the Queen's lover . . .

Her hands continued the rhythmic movements, never faltering. Never allowing the strong surge of emotion to surface; to make its presence felt in anything but the quickening of her heartbeats. Had his hands caressed these shoulders? Had they touched her neck? Her arms? Her breast? Had the Queen permitted him into her bed? To make love to her? Mary felt nauseous at the thought.

'Thank you, my dear.' Elizabeth smiled wanly, shadows under her eyes denoting the fatigue she still suffered. 'I shall retire to bed and Sidney can read to me a while.'

Warming-pans smoothed the linen to a welcome warmth before the crimson and gold covers were turned down. There would be no lover tonight, and Mary, suddenly seeing the Queen through new eyes realized for the first time just how lonely that position could be. Elizabeth too was alone. As alone and lonely as Mary Fytton. Both human. Both needing love. And both apparently having reasons for repudiating men.

The Queen did not improve. Kit Hatton sat untidily in a highbacked chair, fiddling with his buckle, then his dagger, and then morosely trying to remove a smudge from the knee of his hose with a gob of spit. It had been a long night with sleep impossible, and an even longer day of whispered conversations and grimly shaken heads. For once, poise had deserted him and he felt as crumpled and soiled as he would after a night in the stews. But no willing female had reduced him to this sorry state. Quite the reverse. A female as unwilling as any could be. Why had Mary stayed with the Queen? Why hadn't she left when Robert's sister had taken charge and sent the others away? Cat Ashley and Blanche Parry sat in another corner, silent worry lining their faces. But at least they were away from infection. Robert Dudley's interminable pacing was becoming an irritation. Kit bit back the words. They were all in the same predicament and Robert must be in an agony of indecision over what to do if Elizabeth died. What would any of them do? With no undisputed heir, there would be all sorts of upheavals and today's favourites could so easily become tomorrow's victims. Especially if the Scottish queen pressed her claim with the backing of a Catholic army. Robert must be feeling his chances of ever becoming king slipping away from him with Elizabeth Tudor's life. Damn fate! And the devil take reluctant women! Uncertainty had Kit biting his fingernails jagged. What was going on behind the closed door of the bedchamber?

Merging into the warm shadows cast by flickering firelight, Mary Fytton had watched as Lady Sidney supported the Queen so that

Meg Clifford could encourage some special liquid down the royal throat. The dark-coloured potion had taken some time to prepare from an old recipe, but Meg swore that it was the Queen's only hope. Certainly the doctors seemed to have given up and for hours had done nothing but forecast doom. Now Elizabeth appeared to be in a stupor and all they could do was pray that the ancient remedy, handed on to Meg by Mary's old nurse, Elizabeth Fytton, would work one of the miracles for which that old woman was once famous. It had been rumoured that she was a witch and Mary was quite prepared to believe it. Elizabeth Fytton had been responsible for a great deal more than potions in her time. Where would Mary have been without her? Certainly not here. Dead, in all probability!

A steady thrum of rain on the darkened window made the heat and comfort of the fire-corner a welcome luxury, even in the worry of the sickroom, and after an arduous day of fetch and carry Mary's eyes closed wearily. The early childhood days of her life were vague and hazy; days of gathering flowers in sunny meadows and chasing, wild and free, around a cobbled yard. And then she had seen the Queen ride by. Not this queen. Queen Mary. The Papist! And that was when things had begun to change. Her mother's Bible had been put away out of sight, if not out of mind.

Mistress Fytton had insisted that she still recite her lessons. But secretly! It seemed that her parents, both of the New Faith, had extracted a binding promise from the old woman. Mary would follow them in their faith. All the secrecy should have ended with Queen Mary's death. In a religious sense, it did, but the new queen, Elizabeth, felt threatened on all sides, seeing claimants to the throne in every corner.

'Your name is Mary Fytton, child.' The Queen had paused to let this piece of information sink in. 'If you value your freedom . . . If you value your life . . . you will never forget that it is truly your name. And to be certain that you never do forget, I shall keep you close to me. You understand?'

Mary had been only too willing to understand. It was her rightful place. At the Queen's side! The kitchen at Littlecote was hardly the place for one of her birth and breeding even had she not been forced to leave in such unpleasant circumstances. It was only later that she realized what the promise was to mean. No one would ever know her true identity. The likes of that upstart Hatton wouldn't realize the necessity of rising to far greater heights than his present station afforded before he could expect a smile from her. And even then it would be all he could expect! Mary had noticed when he heard news of the Queen's illness how his hand had risen automatically to his brow. The first movement in making the sign of the cross. She suspected he was still a Papist at heart, and that was one thing she could not stomach. But if Elizabeth died, and that other Catholic Mary, Queen of Scotland, became the ruler of the land . . . What then? Mister Hatton would no doubt show his true colours then . . .

Low murmurings aroused Mary from her drowsy, half-asleep thoughts and opening her eyes she was startled to see the tapestried walls blackened by huge shadows; a flock of ravens, birds of death, hovering around the great bed, waiting to pounce. Fear froze her. A nerve twitched in her eyelid. Was Elizabeth dead? Was this the sign? And then her eyes began to focus in the feeble light. Faces wavered into view: William Cecil, Thomas Howard, Nicholas Bacon . . . They were all there . . . the ravens . . . waiting.

'. . . Lord Robert Dudley twenty thousand pounds each year . . . Lord Protector of the Realm . . .'

She could barely hear the Queen's words. The end must be very near. Mary's fear became almost panic. What would become of her? Where would she go? The only answer was marriage . . . Or death. The thought of marriage made the thought of death seem almost pleasant. Unless Robert . . .? If she told him who she was . . .?

At that moment Robert steered his sister away from the crowd around the bed and stood before the fire, not noticing Mary, tucked cosily in her corner.

'The truth, sister. Will she live? I have to know! If she doesn't there are plans to be made immediately. Not a moment to lose. God pray she does for it will take a lot of skill and a good measure of luck to get as close to the Scottish queen. Or opt for a war with Scotland in support of Katherine Grey and her husband Edward, Earl of Hertford.'

'She might. We have been dosing her with a special potion made to the word of King Henry's old healer, Elizabeth Fytton. But ask Meg Clifford. She has seen it work before and can give you a better account of the progress.'

Mary Fytton saw her friend cross the room as Lady Sidney beckoned.

'Well?'

Tension made words scarce. Meg, wide-eyed with responsibility, nodded. 'I think she will live.'

'Think! Only think! Don't you know?' Robert wanted positive answers.

'She will live.' Meg sounded calmer than she felt. And more confident. 'If she doesn't, then I shall make myself a cordial which will see me in heaven before her, its effects are so quick.'

Robert almost smiled. 'So whether she lives or dies you will prove your skill with remedies. Hmm! Another reason to wish the Queen well! And should I ever need such services in the future, may I call on you? Such knowledge as yours can sometimes be an invaluable friend.'

'I am your servant, sir, and always shall be. As my husband, Lord Strange, will vouchsafe.'

Mary shivered in the heat as Meg curtseyed to Robert and his sister. The murmured conversation had an almost sinister overtone. As though some pact had been made. And then the group beside the bed began to move and file out of the room. It seemed that business with the Queen was over and the three beside the fire moved to join the exodus. Only then did Mary rise from the shadows to stand, listening to the shuffling feet, the rain on the windows, and the settling of the logs as they burnt in the hearth.

'Mistress.'

She nearly jumped out of her skin. Christopher Hatton took hold of her arm and slid his hand around her waist.

'Come out of this room for a while. You look exhausted and there are others who can take their turn. Please. You will make yourself ill and be of no use to anyone.' Trying to coax her towards the door he dared a little pressure on the bodice of her gown; felt her warmth through the cloth and the suppleness of flesh as she pulled away. She was made for love. She was made for him, and if, as she had insinuated, only the Queen stood between them, then the way was almost clear. She could not pretend to him that Mary, Queen of Scots, would have any objection to his suit. 'Don't reject me now. I am worried for your safety and all I want is to take you out for fresh air.'

Lies! All lies. All he wanted, if he told the truth, was to bed her. To feel her respond to his lovemaking; to feel her rise to meet him on a wave of pure emotion. To break through that barrier of haughty reserve and tread virgin ground . . .

'Leave, sir, I know your intentions, and even if I were in sore need of a protector I should look higher than a penniless squire to escort me, even as far as the door.'

'Oh Mary. My sweet Mary. How high must I climb before I am worthy of notice? Put a name to that pinnacle and I shall conquer it. I will do anything to prove my love.' Kit lifted her hand to his mouth to kiss her fingers. She was trembling.

'You already go too far sir, but if you would really know the truth my future depends on a Knight of the Garter.' She mentioned no name in particular but saw immediately that she had startled him. The brilliant sapphire eyes held a quizzical expression as his mouth quirked in a smile, half questioning. Without a word he asked what she thought her credentials might be that she could expect so influential a champion. But the answer to that she was not at liberty to tell him.

'Then a Knight of the Garter I shall be.' Pulling her swiftly into his arms in the privacy of the darkened corner he all but bruised her mouth with a fierce and hungry kiss. It was worth the resounding slap across the face with which he was rewarded. Kit chuckled indulgently. 'Vixen! One day I shall tame you. One day, when I have persuaded the Queen that I am worthy of the honour you require me to have. But I shall do it even if I have to prostitute myself in the cause.'

Cheeks flushed angrily, and eyes sparking hate, Mary swept past him just as a commotion started outside the door. She hesitated.

'I tell you it is the only way.' The thick Germanic tones of Doctor Burcot were unmistakable. 'If all else has failed, what is there to lose. Come on! Come on!'

This last was snapped impatiently at two young apprentices who seemed to be carrying a bolt of cloth between them. As indeed they were. Lord Robert Dudley, Knight of the Garter, and his sister, Mary Sidney, looked perplexed.

'But surely it would be wrong to move Her Majesty in her extremity?' Lady Sidney did not know what the Queen would say about such an idea. The leading apprentice nearly tripped over his long student cloak in the dismal light, filtered now by smoke and fumes from the torches and fire. Only fear of his master kept him on his feet. That, and a steadying hand from his fellow student.

'Clumsy dolt! Am I surrounded by idiots?'

Burcot clipped him about the ear. 'Leave that now and fetch the mattress.'

The two youngsters scurried out, returning almost instantly with a mattress which they laid before the fire.

'More wood! Get that fire blazing.'

The doctor was used to giving orders in such circumstances. And used to having them instantly obeyed! There was no shortage of willing hands and within minutes the Queen was wrapped in yards of fleecy red cloth and found herself lying rather strangely on a mattress in front of the fire.

'May I?' Meg Clifford stepped forward with a cup of her special remedy in her hand.

'What is it?' Burcot took the cup and sniffed at the contents. 'Ah, the tisane! What is in it exactly?'

Meg rattled off the list of ingredients, some of which sounded positively noxious to the uninitiated. The doctor nodded approvingly. 'Yes, yes.' He bent over the prone form lying at his feet and lifted her head so that she could sip the liquid. Whether it was the drink or the doctor's manner which comforted the Queen no one knew but from that moment she seemed to rest easier.

Until, that is, Elizabeth lifted her hand to wipe the sweat which was beginning to bead her brow. She began wailing like a child.

'Get these people out of here. They shall not see me disfigured!'

Lady Sidney tried unsuccessfully to calm her mistress.

'It would be best if you left.' She looked nervously at her brother. How would he feel about the Queen if she became raddled and pockmarked? Would the glitter of the Crown be enough to blind him to such hideousness? It would have to be, and she knew Robert well enough to realize that power meant more to him than prettiness. Mister Hatton and the likes might not find honeyed compliments dripping from their tongues quite so readily though!

'Ppht!' The doctor dismissed the purplish swellings with an impatient wave of the hand. 'The spots? Or death? Which would you prefer? Is it not better to suffer the spot? Should I have left them inside to poison you? Ah! I am a fool! I even thought to look for thanks!'

Elizabeth was suitably chastened and in the event, the disfigurement she so dreaded did not come to pass. Her dear friend Mary Sidney was not so lucky. Some days later she too succumbed to the disease and her face became so scarred that she asked the Queen's permission to retire to a quiet life in the country where she could devote herself to the welfare of her children.

The gap left in Elizabeth's world by the departure of her lifelong friend, Mary Sidney, would not be easily filled. There were other women to wait on her and do her bidding; older maids who had nursed her from being a child, like dear Blanche Parry and her darling Cat Ashley. But Mary had grown up with her; the Dudley brothers, Ambrose, Robert and Henry had joined with Mary in showing the family loyalty to Elizabeth's cause; and her husband, Henry Sidney had shown his friendship as much as any of them. Elizabeth sighed. How often did God have to demonstrate that she stood alone? That she must be strong and independent? At least this lovely child, this other Mary, had not caught the terrible illness which marred so many lives. She watched as the girl helped to lay out the garments in which the Queen would sleep. A quiet young woman. Fortunately! If she had ever shown signs of having inherited one fraction of her father's ambitious nature it would have been a very different story. There were those who entered the Tower never to be seen again. And that would have been a great pity. Mary may have more of her mother's placid ways, but not her features. In her face she was the image of her father. Oh, how she reminded Elizabeth of that man! He would never be dead whilst Mary lived.

'Mary.' The girl looked up at the sound of the Queen's voice, a dimple, low on her left cheek endowing her with a charming look of innocence. The same charm he had exercised, though not so innocently. 'Come. Braid my hair, and then you may soothe my aching shoulders as only you know how.' Elizabeth dismissed the other women. 'The strain of the last few weeks has told on you Cat. And indeed on all of you. I shall be glad for you to retire to your own beds and leave me to mine. Mistress Fytton will sleep in the closet in case I have need of help during the night.'

Mary set about the tasks, carefully braiding handfuls of the long red-gold curls. Attractive hair. Bright and soft. And something else . . . A sensual quality which made her want to run her fingers through it endlessly; bury her face in its perfumed depths and suffocate with the pleasure of it . . . Mary's heart pounded loudly in the ears as such ludicrous thoughts flashed rapidly through her mind. Was she going mad? Pray to God the Queen could not detect these crazy feelings . . . She must be ill. It was the only explanation. And yet Elizabeth's skin, naked shoulders . . .

Mary could feel her legs shaking as she tried to control the devil in her head, tried to halt the tremor in her arms as she massaged her mistress's head and neck . . . as Robert must have often done. Robert had sometimes stayed in these rooms for the best part of the night . . . What else had he done? Was Elizabeth his wife in all but name?

'Are you cold, Mary my dear?' Elizabeth took Mary's hand in hers as it caressed her collarbone. 'You are shaking. Surely not with fear? Come here.'

The Queen rose from the chair and moved to sit on the edge of the great bed, patting a space beside her and smiling at her maid. Mary obeyed, keeping her eyes downcast in case Elizabeth read her mind.

'Look at me, child.'

Slowly Mary raised her head and the Queen was stunned by the poignant expression in the huge dark eyes. That very look had echoed through the years to haunt her dreams on many a lonely night. His eyes had looked at her like that . . . A prelude to those first thrills of adolescence, to the urgency to touch and be touched. This, girl, who had been degraded by a brute of a man, an animal, was pouring out all her emotion in a girlish infatuation for her mistress. Her Queen. And she was *his* daughter . . . A miracle! An accident of birth which some would choose to use against Elizabeth as they had tried to use Jane Grey in her sister's reign. As they had tried to use Katherine Grey only recently. Damn Katherine Grey for marrying a Seymour. And producing a son into the bargain!

Then the Queen smiled softly to herself. Mary was in no frame of mind to be running off with ambitious courtiers and producing sons. After the affair with Mister Darrel, it was the last thing she would be doing. But those eyes! His exactly. It was as though he still looked at her; wanting her; loving her.

Slowly Elizabeth put out a hand to touch the girl's pink-and-white complexion and as she did so a single, glistening teardrop rolled silently, hopelessly, down onto the royal fingers.

'Don't, Mary. Don't cry. I understand. Truly I do. I too am alone and may not marry. Indeed, I do not want to marry. I want only to see men wanting me. To show me their weakness by desiring me. I like to see them warmed by the flames in their loins, not dampened by the quenching. Besides, if a man rules my body then it follows that he rules England with it.

'No need to weep, my love. We are as God made us, and for a reason, though that reason may be obscure.'

The Queen leaned gently towards the girl and softly kissed the tear-stained face. Her cheeks; her eyes; and then the trembling wet lips. Mary felt the tenderness held out to her in the hands which encircled her waist as, sobbing with relief, she returned the kisses two for one.

* * *

'You have a deadly aim.' Robert Dudley watched the flight of the arrow keenly. He never ceased to be surprised at the hidden strength of the Queen's favourite dancing partner and was constantly reminding himself that the devil came in many disguises. The young man seemed open enough in his dealings, but Robert was not prepared to leave anything to chance. There were certain men in his pay who could be relied upon to give a good account of Mister Hatton's movements. Day or night.

'Would that my love-darts found their mark as easily!' Kit had lately been giving a lot of thought to his intentions towards Mary Fytton. What was the fascination? Initially, the black hair and flashing eyes had reminded him of that first heady taste of manhood in the arms of his wild gipsy-girl. But what now? Now that he knew how superficial those similarities were? Why did her constant refusals torment him? It wasn't as though he found that difficulty in other quarters. Quite the opposite in fact, and he had often had to caution the ladies in question in case the Queen took objection. His flattery of Her Majesty bordered on the ridiculous at times, but she loved to be surrounded by handsome men praising her beauty. What others did in moderation, Kit was prepared to do in the extreme. If it would one day lead to him being created Knight of the Garter!

'Perhaps she already has a lover.' Tom Heneage took careful aim at the butts.

'No, I shouldn't think so.' Robert disagreed. 'She's too solemn and far too proud to spread her legs for any man before bringing him to book. And marriage is anyway the quickest way to fall from favour with our darling queen. All Kit's muscle isn't in his arm, is it? There's enough in his head to control those thrusting thighs! Eh, Kit?' There were plenty of females, away from the rules of the Court, who would relieve him of his pent-up frustrations. 'Where to tonight?'

Kit grinned as he tested the bowstring against his shoulder.

'The Three Tuns.' He aimed confidently at the target, pulling his arm back strongly and smoothly. The Court was at Windsor. 'A group of travelling players is in town and we have arranged a small entertainment.' He let loose the arrow, hitting the target dead centre once more. 'And supper afterwards!'

'Ah, would that I could join you!' Robert slapped his back by way of congratulation for the shot. 'But Cecil has arrived and there are things which must be discussed.'

Tom Heneage raised an eyebrow. 'The succession? Again?'

'Aye, again. And again and again if I know Elizabeth. She is as willing to nominate an heir as she is to marry. Me, or anyone else.' He would have much preferred the Three Tuns, but business was business, and Robert still had high hopes that the Queen would keep the promise she had made to marry him. One day soon.

'Speaking of whom . . .' Kit nodded across

the park. 'Is it the Queen?' He squinted into the winter sunshine, thinking that his eyes were deceiving him.

It was. And accompanied by three of her young maids, but dressed so strangely that the onlookers couldn't help but stare. Gone were the trappings of royalty. Gone the expensive furs and velvets which normally kept the chill winds from Elizabeth's pale skin. All four women were dressed as simple country girls. Dairymaids or flower-girls or some such. And happily laughing and chattering as though it was the first day of Spring rather than the twenty-sixth day of November.

'Your Majesty.' The men at the butts bowed before approaching the women.

'It is always a pleasure to see Your Majesty, but if I may venture to be so bold, rarely have I seen you look so lovely. Simply charming.' Robert bent to kiss the proffered hand. 'Is it a game? Must we do likewise?'

The Queen laughed gaily, catching Mary Fytton's hand in hers as she did so and smiling at the young girl with delight. Kate Carey and Anne Russell followed suit and for a moment Kit Hatton thought that they were going to join in a circle for some country dance or other as he once had at Holdenby. He couldn't take his eyes from Mary Fytton's face. She looked radiant. He had never hoped to see her so happy with life. Not until he made her so, at any rate! Who had done this to her? Was Tom right? Had she found herself a lover after all? And if so, who? Kit felt an iron band of jealousy tighten around his heart. Which lucky man had managed to breach those formidably held defences? God's death! If he ever found out who had done it he would not be answerable for his actions. He would cut him limb from limb. And worse. He would cut him off from such pleasures once and for all!

'You think we act a part? Perhaps we do, but do we act today, or was it yesterday we spoke the lines we had learnt? I have been cast in the role of queen, this I admit, and I play it as well as I am able. But sometimes I yearn to be myself and last night I discovered just how easy that can be.' Elizabeth smiled at them fondly. 'Don't tell me that you, three of my favourite men, never do what is expected of you, rather than what you really wish? Don't we all act out our parts?'

The protestations were loud and long.

'You are cruel, Your Majesty. We are as you see us. Your loyal servants until death. Servants who would die for you. Servants who die each time you frown on us for some small mistake or slight misdemeanour.'

'As pretty with your speeches as ever.' She patted Robert's hand playfully. 'I don't doubt that you love your queen, but what of the woman?' The Queen was suddenly serious. 'And when I am that woman . . . when I am myself, I have gone beyond your understanding. Beyond the pale!'

* * *

'Your very good health, sirs.' Robert Dudley raised his cup to the company. 'Drink your fill and I shall pay. Reward for a fine entertainment.'

The Boar's Head was full to bursting and this news was received with cheers and thanks out of all proportion to the gift. Most of the customers, gaily clad, arm-waving and highly vociferous, were members of the acting fraternity, or would-be actors hanging awestruck on every observation of their idols, each and every one of them striving to catch the attention of a crowd. The result was kaleidoscopic chaos.

'And we in turn salute you, sir.' The huge form of a white-clad Greek god, gilded laurel leaves askew now on his yellow wig, swept off the cloak of the West Wind standing beside him to make an exaggerated bow. 'Nor do we forget the benefactor whose words put an end to our dumb-show. Gentlemen, I give you Mister Hatton.'

To further ear-splitting applause and slopped ale from raised cups Kit acknowledged his part in the afternoon's events, smiling as the serving wenches prepared to make the most of the good humour and attendant goodwill which invariably followed these perormances.

'Would that I could pay to keep them here a while longer, but as usual, not only are my pockets empty, but I am indebted to my tailor, my shoemaker . . . and my wine merchant!' Kit raised the goblet to his mouth. A man had to keep up appearances if he wished to remain at the Queen's side, but Her Majesty seemed to think that her courtiers were magicians, producing money out of thin air. It was as well that he could take his mind from such trivial annoyances in more relaxed company than the Queen's Presence Chamber afforded. The pox take Mary Fytton for finding other arms more amenable than his! The effort may be crippling him financially but he would show her! One day he would become a Knight of the Garter and though she pleaded with him on bended knee, though she sobbed and tore her hair, he would throw her taunts back in her face. Refuse to lower himself for such a woman. Or so he told himself.

'Aye. I think I'll have my own company of players one of these fine days. And when I do, will you still write for me?' Robert's mind wasn't fully occupied by the riotous jocularity going on around him. Kit had provided the entertainment to take his friend's thoughts from other problems. And he had almost, but not quite, succeeded. The plump breasts of the ale-wife's assistant undulated with laughter as she teased the young lad, still dressed as a girl from his part in the play, about the static nature of his wooden paps.

'He'll do for me though!' The bronzed skin and faded hair of the speaker told their own tale of sun and wind; and the sinewy arms had regular knowledge of coarse rope and canvas sail. The seaman slung one arm casually around the boy's narrow shoulders. 'You wouldn't say no to a healthy young fellow with a pocket full of silver now? Would you?'

'That's where my money will be going in a few months' time.' Robert Dudley leaned towards Kit, pointing his finger at the sailor as he enticed the boy-actor away from the serving wench. 'Hawkins brought in a handsome cargo and those who were wise enough to invest in the expedition have made a fine profit. He is eager to sail again, if he can get a new ship in addition to the refitting he hopes to do on his own. Elizabeth has promised that one will be forthcoming and I for one shall gamble on the venture.'

'Elizabeth has promised?' Kit raised a cynical eyebrow.

'Hmmmph. You're right, of course, but there is more likelihood of her keeping a promise to Hawkins than one made to me.'

That statement, plus the fact that the entertainment was now over, brought his problems with Elizabeth back to mind.

'But this time she has gone too far! Not only will she not marry me, but she has the impertinence to offer me to another woman.'

'Not just another woman, surely? A queen. And if Elizabeth is thinking of her cousin Mary as a suitable wife for her darling Robin then it follows that she thinks her a suitable heir to the throne of England. So Elizabeth offers you her throne, but not her body, and unless those who have seen the Scottish queen lie, the body she does offer you will be recompense in itself. They say she is a real beauty.' Kit wouldn't have had many objections to becoming King of Scotland, given the chance.

'But why? Last year she said she would give me her answer by Christmas. Then she would tell me by Candlemas. Now she gives me away as a gift. A bauble. A puppy-dog! She has changed. There are no more playful nights spent trying to persuade her with passionate kisses and caresses which would have melted any ice-maiden but that one. Now it is goodnight at the door and a woman to undress her. Young Mistress Fytton as like as not.'

'Don't talk to me about that one.' Kit rolled his eyes to the ceiling despairingly. 'I thought she had taken a lover but all my enquiries so far have revealed nothing. One day . . . One day I shall have that little beauty if it's the last thing I ever do! But for now, it's Wood Street through to Cripplegate . . . and Silver Street. If you have a mind for willing arms, slender legs, and a romp which will end in the sleep of exhaustion!'

Such interludes, they both realized, kept them sane in the mad world of the Court where they walked the knife-edge. The Queen's favourites today; tomorrow, ruined men with no credit from even the lowest quality merchant in town. Yet even these short forays into normality must be kept secret from the virgin Queen. Above all, a favourite must be faithful!

*　　*　　*

'The man sets out to infuriate me!'

Elizabeth certainly looked furious, pacing the floor and twisting the great seal round and round on her finger.

'He goes off without permission. Again! I never know where he is or what he is doing half the time . . . Quarantine, of all things! He should have had more sense than to rush off to Ambrose the minute he returned. He knew why the troops were recalled. How many had we lost to the filthy disease? And now he puts himself in danger of catching the plague!' The Queen scanned the letter again, as if in disbelief.

Mary Fytton hurriedly poured a cup of the soothing infusion, freshly made by Meg Clifford. It was invaluable at times like these. The two gentlewomen exchanged a knowing glance. It was no wonder that so many rumours ran through the Court before becoming general knowledge to the Queen's subjects when she demonstrated her personal affection for Robert Dudley in this manner. To Mary's discomfort, Elizabeth caught the glance.

'What is it? What are they saying now?'

Mary hesitated.

'Speak, Mistress. Speak!' The Queen was in no mood for procrastination. 'Or it will be the worse for you.'

Mary knew the Queen's strength and domination and understood perfectly that she would be punished privately if she didn't tell the truth. She fell to her knees in an obeisance indicating rather more submission than was normal from one in daily contact with the Queen. Meg busied herself on the other side of the room, keeping well out of the discussion.

'They say . . .' Mary cleared her throat and started again. 'They say that you are to have a child and that Robert has been sent away in disgrace. Or that he has run away in fear!'

'Ha! So I am with child again, am I? How many is this? Five? Six? And what do you say, Mary?' The Queen's voice softened perceptibly. 'What do you say?'

'The very thought of those crude people discussing Your Majesty's health in such a way sickens me. Such things should be kept private.'

'They may gossip all they wish, Mary dear, but the truth about my health . . . shall remain as always, very private.'

As the Queen raised her from her knees Mary saw that all the anger had evaporated and feeling the slight but definite pressure of Elizabeth's fingers on her hand, smiled.

'It is as well that they think me enamoured . . . of Robin . . . And it would suit my purposes if he thought the same . . . He is a very dear friend . . . Mmmm . . .'

On the first day of September, Robert Dudley was declared free from any suspicion of having contracted the plague and later in the same month Elizabeth made him a magnificent gift. The castle and parkland of Kenilworth. Sparkling streams fed the dammed mere, a broad pool of water almost as imposing as the faded red of the castle itself. His fears were allayed. Elizabeth had not cast him off. There was still hope.

CHAPTER FOUR

Leaving Queen's College by way of Silver Street before turning left towards Trinity, Kit Hatton sauntered slowly in the late afternoon sun, thumbs thrust absentmindedly under his leather belt and eyes focused sightlessly on the advancing ground three feet ahead of him. His brain felt as though it was made of moss; a damp, furry sponge, completely incapable of thought. How, in God's name, did Elizabeth do it? The woman was inexhaustible? For four days, since the minute they had arrived in Cambridge, life had consisted entirely of receptions and orations, endless monologues and dissertations, mountains of food served at continual banquets, followed by all manner of intellectual entertainments. And the Queen not missing a single word of it! Kit couldn't say the same for himself. Yet the visit had started out so well.

The Queen had looked magnificent as she rode into the courtyard of the college, slim and elegant, and perfectly at ease on horseback. Dressed in rich black velvet relieved only by a delicate filigree of embroidered gold thread, and with that striking red-gold hair caught in a matching golden net she had been every inch a queen. Sunbeams had turned the spangled feathers of her hat into a glittering crown as she nodded appreciatively, listening intently to the torrent of Latin with which she was being greeted. But the tingle of excitement he felt had nothing at all to do with Elizabeth. Its cause stood silently beside him, clad becomingly in rose-coloured silk trimmed sparingly with silver lace. Thank God she couldn't see the effect she had on him! No one else in the world had the power to make him feel so gauche and immature. It was ridiculous.

It was embarrassing! And he knew she must have felt his hand tremble on her elbow as he escorted her behind the Queen to the King's Chapel.

Standing beside Mistress Fytton as choirboys sang with the voices of angels and the sun scattered a profusion of sapphire and ruby jewels through stained-glass windows into the congregation, was the nearest to heaven Christopher Hatton had ever been. How he held back from grasping her hand he never knew. Except that her disdain would have spoilt the moment. Still, he dared to glance at her several times, seeing that her eyes were modestly lowered and her thoughts on anything but him. But on leaving that hallowed place she had spurned him once more, offering her arm to none other than that pretty boy, Henry Darnley. Kit had been furious. It must surely have been a calculated insult on her part. She couldn't actually like Henry . . .

Passing the end of Trinity Lane Kit automatically felt in his purse for a small coin. The blind beggar blessed him as it clinked pleasingly into the bowl at his feet.

'Count your blessings, Hatton, you fool!' God had made him sound in mind and limb and Lady Luck had seen fit to lead him into the path of Elizabeth Tudor, a queen who loved nothing more than being surrounded by handsome flatterers. What more could any sane man ask for? Why was he not content with his lot? And now that he came to think about it, he was not the only one with problems. Robert was still smarting from the knowledge that Elizabeth was willing to offer him to her cousin. Why? What had got into the women of this Court? It seemed that they were trying to do without men altogether. There were those who thought that women were unfit to rule, but these days there was no obvious alternative. Mary, Queen of Scots was most definitely a woman! Only time would tell which would be the stronger in matters of State but Mary would have to prove herself more than an ordinary mortal to better Elizabeth of England when it came to handling men. *She* had the happy knack of making them grovel willingly at her feet for a smile though they had been kicked twice around the room in as many minutes, and with as much respect as might be shown to a pig's bladder. And her stamina this week had left men reeling. Cecil had given in to his gout days ago. Robert had his work cut out for him and no mistake! Kit sighed. Were there always problems where there were women?

A sudden swarm of gnats appeared from nowhere, dancing delicately about his ears and nose as they examined each orifice minutely, and keeping perfect pace with him in the balmy evening air. Flapping his hands at them achieved nothing as the insects determined to know him better, until he finally resorted to removing his cap and flailing it wildly around his head, cursing and swearing in the crude expletives usually reserved for the scum of the stews as they bled his pockets dry. Damn the beasts. He'd be cobbled all over with itchy bumps by morning!

The suppressed giggles startled him. Looking around Kit realized that his feet had meandered as far out of their way as his thoughts. They had taken him well past his lodgings, through the town and out to Midsummer Meadow. He had to smile. The girl was right. He must have looked like an overdressed village idiot, prancing across the grass waving his hat madly around in the air. Still, he was no idiot when it came to appreciating a comely figure! The girl was perhaps seventeen, he thought, well developed inside the tightness of the laced bodice but less so in her confidence with men. The laughter had escaped her involuntarily and she had tried to stifle it with fingers which were neither pampered nor ill-treated, rather than allow it freedom to attract his attention. Kit turned and approached her slowly and steadily, pretending a frown without trying to disguise the twinkle in his eyes.

'You think it comical to watch me being eaten alive? Wretched wench! I shall have to teach you a lesson you won't forget in a hurry!'

The laughter stopped and the smile it left behind quivered slightly with nervous apprehension. She had been watching him since his emergence from the backdrop of huddled buildings across the meadow, obviously lost in thought and completely unconscious of his direction. Had he gone much further he would have ended up to his neck in the River Cam. And that would have been a terrible waste of expensive clothing. He had to be a courtier. Someone who was on close terms with Her Majesty. Who else would be able to afford a suit of pearl-grey velvet cut with lilac silk? Silk hose too, and a pair of boots made in hunting style, but of such fine dyed leather that they must surely be just for show. Perhaps courtiers had no sense of humour!

'I'm sorry, sir. I saw no wild beasts snapping at your heels and therefore thought you in no danger. We live very simply at home and I thought I was a witness to some new court dance. Forgive my ignorance, sir.' The girl dipped in a perfect curtsey.

Was she still laughing at him then? Impudent madam! Perhaps she was not so innocent after all!

'Then who are you, simple maid?' Kit took her hand and raised it to his mouth. Ringless. But clean. Not the hand of one who habitually hung about the meadow looking for custom.

'Nan Hobson, sir. I live with my father and brother over at the livery stables in the town. In fact they would be angry with me if they realized that I was out alone at evening.' She made as if to pull away, but her hand was still captive. A fluttering heart told her she should leave, whilst at the same time it insisted that she stay. He didn't look evil. Or heartless. Or cruel.

She smiled up at him shyly only to find herself gazing helplessly into the bluest pair of eyes she had ever seen. Bluer than the summer sky. Bluer than cornflowers. And not without humour at all.

'Oh . . .' It was almost a sigh. Almost a moan. With a well-practised look of tender compassion laced with impish mischief Kit rooted her to the spot.

'So, Nan Hobson . . .' He lingered over the name, 'Why are you out alone?'

'I escaped, sir. With Her Majesty here they are so busy . . .' She faltered as he came close enough for her to feel the warmth of his breath against her cheek; to smell the faint masculine odour of his skin.

'You too?' By his sympathetic smile she understood that he was not in his rightful place at that moment either, which somehow made them partners in crime; miscreant absconders from authority.

Feeling his arms encompass her waist, Nan made the required show of protest but it was obvious to Kit that the action was mere formality and in no way designed to make him hesitate. Yet he would swear she was still a virgin. He could see it in her face, the eyes wide with awed wonder and a very kissable little mouth which trembled with expectant hope. Gently then. And with feeling.

Nan had seen courtiers come and go through the streets of Cambridge all her life and she had dreamed the silly romantic dreams of young girls everywhere. One day the most handsome courtier of them all would appear on her doorstep and carry her away from life in a straw-strewn yard where horses dominated everything and the steaming pile of dung in the corner perfumed the house, her clothes, and even the food she ate. And here he was! More handsome than even her dreams had promised.

The first touch of his mouth against hers made her catch her breath. As though she had suddenly been plunged into cold water. How could a kiss be so strong yet so tender at the same time? The firm pressure of his body caused her knees to buckle under her and before she knew what was happening Kit had laid her carefully down on the grass in the shelter of a small cluster of hazel bushes.

'My sweet, sweet Nan. My love. My angel.' He kissed her ear, her neck, and then her mouth once more, this time with a controlled urgency, letting her feel his increasing hunger; his mounting desire. Petticoats had never proved to be an obstacle in such circumstances and Kit was delighted to feel her shiver expectantly as he coolly slid his hand into the private warmth of her smooth young thighs. With the most delicate of caresses he induced sensations calculated to heighten her newly discovered awareness; to give promise of the fulfilment yet to come. Nan clung to him, wide-eyed and eager as he entered with the utmost care and consideration. And then her body took control. Responding instinctively to the pulsating rhythms. Arching her back and winding her legs around his to keep him safe inside. And Kit re-lived, through Nan's breathless loss of innocence, his own ecstatic initiation; his own awakening in the half-light of dawn on Coneybury Hill.

'Happy?' Kit moved a wayward lock of hair from her cheek and tucked it under her cap. Her thick, dark lashes were dew-kissed with the merest trace of tears. He wiped them away with a finger. 'I didn't hurt you?'

'No . . . Oh no.' The pert little nose wrinkled with anxiety. 'It was . . . It was . . .' He stopped her search for words with a kiss.

If only Mary Fytton would look at him like that. If only she would condescend to look at him at all! For four days she had deliberately tormented him by flinging herself at Darnley. Why? Because she really adored the simpering popinjay? Or because the lad had royal blood in his veins? Or simply to throw Christopher Hatton deeper into the black pit of despair which yawned between them? Nan Hobson, scarcely more than a child, could give Mistress Fytton lessons on how to respond to a man's advances. Instead, Mary chose to stick to Lord Darnley as tenaciously as shit to a blanket.

'Sir . . .' Nan interrupted his thoughts.

'Mmmm?' Kit stroked her unlaced paps absentmindedly.

'May I know your name?'

His chuckle became a laugh which convulsed him for so long that he ended by wiping tears from his own eyes. Sweet baby. She didn't even know his name!

'Indeed you may. It is little enough reward for the service you have done me.' The tension in his neck had eased and his angry, muddled brain was once more beginning to think in a logical manner. Standing, he bowed low before her. As low as he did before the Queen herself. 'Christopher Hatton, at your service, Mistress. Gentleman to Her Majesty Queen Elizabeth, and a gentleman who was in sore need of a diversion from his worries. I thank you from the bottom of my heart and assure you that so long as I live I shall not forget my little Nan.'

'I . . . I shan't see you again?' There was disappointment in her voice, and tears in her eyes.

'I'm sorry. We leave tomorrow to make our way back to London. Where the Queen goes, I must follow.'

'Oh.' Her voice wavered with the unshed

tears. She couldn't trust herself to speak. Silently she turned towards the town, glimmering now with lantern-light and candle. She should have been home hours ago. She should never have come out at all!

Parting, for Nan, was bitter-sweet as she turned, bewildered, towards home, and a thrashing. The long hot hours of the summer night would be filled with fleabites and the sickly, steaming odour of the stableyard. A commonplace night. Except for the memories of her one brief taste of heaven; her fool's paradise which would have her sobbing uncontrollably into the lumpy stubble of her straw pallet.

Kit, on the other hand, swung jauntily down King Street in the direction of his lodgings, whistling as he went. Things were never as bad as they seemed, he decided, and perhaps if he kept his eyes and ears open he might find a way to come between Mistress Fytton and her pretty paramour. All he asked was half a chance!

With the Court back in London, Christopher Hatton waited for a way of achieving this small ambition. The arrival of James Melville, the Scottish queen's envoy, had Robert Dudley making himself scarce, finding it very convenient to look over Hawkin's new ship, the *Jesus of Lubeck*, before his investment sailed for warmer climes. If the subject of his proposed marriage to Mary,

Queen of Scots was to come under discussion he wanted to be well away from it. But Kit found that Elizabeth was in no great hurry to get down to politics immediately. First her curiosity about her cousin, famed for her beauty, had to be satisfied. Did Mary play? How did she dress? And in the dance?

Melville persevered. Perhaps the Earl of Bedford and Lord Robert could meet the Earls of Lethington and Murray on the borders . . .? Kit, attendant in Robert's absence, listened as the Queen parried the dour Scotman's searching questions, determined to prove herself more beautiful, witty and adroit, but above all, more feminine than any woman in the world. Especially Mary!

But what was that? Did Melville stress Robert's lack of title amongst so many earls? Did he think Elizabeth offered her cousin a mere nobody as a mate? A nondescript? A common man? Or imagine Lord Robert not well thought of by the Queen of England? Did he think she sent him into exile willingly? Nothing could have been further from the truth. And she would prove it! Lord Robert would be invested as Baron Denbigh, Earl of Leicester.

The news stunned all those in the room. It was the reward Robert had been promised long ago, but Elizabeth had withheld the title from him during one of their little tiffs. Some listeners were pleased; some were apprehensive. In particular, Kit noticed Margaret Douglas's face. Lady Lennox looked as though she had been slapped. Her husband had recently been given leave to visit his estates in Scotland though there were rumours that it was ambition which drove him north. His wife's ambition for her son, Henry Darnley. Kit moved to sit beside her.

'Would she say no to an earl?' Kit kept his voice low.

'Aye, to a Puritan earl!' Margaret almost hissed the words through clenched teeth. 'Mary would never betray her faith.' Her eyes moved to the slender figure of her son. Catholic to the core. And of royal blood! Lady Lennox spat on the Earl of Leicester. Mentally, at any rate.

It wasn't difficult for Kit to read her thoughts. 'You have other hopes?'

Though the words were whispered Margaret shot him a warning glance. She knew that Mister Hatton's religious sympathies lay in her own camp but there were spies everywhere. No one knew how many men William Cecil and Robert Dudley had in their pay.

'If we can only get him to Scotland . . . We are assured that . . .' She left the words unsaid but Kit knew without a doubt that James Melville's true mission had not been to bring hope of an alliance between Queen Mary and Robert. Robert would be relieved. And if

Elizabeth could be persuaded to let Darnley go . . .

Slamming the door of his lodgings in Silver Street behind him, Kit clutched his fur-lined cloak tightly and turned into the icy sword-edge of the wind. This weather was the very devil! It chafed the skin and caused noses to dribble all manner of disgusting emissions. And the Thames had frozen solid. Children slid around on it squealing with a delight which left Kit feeling old as well as cold. The festive season had been a total disaster, the Queen succumbing to a debilitating cold just as the entertainments were about to begin, and not being likely to emerge from her rooms until the New Year. The whole holiday had fallen flat and the Court had merely gone through the motions. There had been no heart in it. At least so far as Kit was concerned. When the Queen was ill Robert hovered around her door. And Mary never left her beside! So now it was off to the Boar's Head and several cups of hot, spiced wine. And the company of friends.

The hoar-frost melted from his beard in seconds before the blaze of split logs crackling in the hearth as Kit leaned back contentedly to watch the dank-smelling steam spiral up from his boots. Would Elizabeth do anything about Darnley? That was the question which kept returning. She might. Anything was possible. He thought back to their conversation. They had spent the greater part of one afternoon practising a new movement in the Queen's favourite dance, the galliard, and Kit had once more fallen foul of his emotions. Mary had refused to partner him, squashing him as though he were a head-louse, and then proceeded to inflame his irritation by treading a measure with that lisping lickspittle, Darnley. His annoyance hadn't shown. He was too astute for that. Instead, he excelled himself in amusing his monarch so that he spent most of the time holding her hand and being told how adorable he was. Christopher Hatton could use his charm on anyone, when the need arose.

'Flatterer.' Elizabeth enjoyed these frivolous interludes when the worries of government could be left lying dormant for a while. 'And you are no mean peasant when it comes to style. Or features.' She smiled pleasantly up into his eyes. 'We make a handsome couple, don't you think?'

Kit sighed dramatically. 'I am not worthy to kiss the ground you tread on. Oh cruel Queen to paint such a picture of bliss, giving the hope where there is none. Would that we were simple lovers like those two happy youngsters.' He nodded to where Mary sat whispering and giggling behind her hand to Henry.

He had watched Elizabeth's eyes narrow thoughtfully as she glanced across at her maid. Only the Queen was allowed to lead men on in a merry dance which never came to anything.

Wanton behaviour amongst her women was not tolerated. Not for a moment. And Mary herself had told him that the Queen would never allow her to marry. Kit was convinced that it was all part of the mystery surrounding the girl. The Queen's ladies always needed permission to marry, but even so, many of them had married and raised families. But not those who might be a threat to the Crown . . . like Katherine Grey . . . a figurehead who could be used by certain factions agains Elizabeth Tudor. After all, there were those who still thought her a bastard . . . Or like Henry, Lord Darnley, grandson of King Henry's sister, Margaret. If Mary posed that kind of threat their the Queen would most definitely not give her permission to marry anyone. And especially not Henry!

'I wonder . . .?' Elizabeth had tapped her forefinger steadily against her chin as she thought, her eyes searching for, and finding, Margaret Douglas. Was that ambitious windbag trying a different attack on the throne now? And what was Mary up to? The answer to that question should not be long in coming. Mistress Fytton would be in close attendance on her mistress for a while. That would keep the little trollop's mind from men. Even from effeminate men!

Kit had felt the Queen's mood change with the steely pressure of her hand. The situation had been brought to her notice. All he could do now was wait. The matter was out of his hands. But would she do anything to remove Darnley from Mary's side?

The wine in his stomach was creating its own glow and his bootleather was becoming nicely crisp in the convivial atmosphere. No sailors in tonight. Hawkins and his fleet of four would be well out of the storm-tossed seas around England and heading for the sun. And gold, the Queen and Robert hoped. If only Kit had been able to throw his hand in with them! Next time. Definitely next time, he promised himself. So actors of varying degrees had the floor to themselves and argument, their stock-in-trade, was by far the noisiest and most common method of communication. Which profession provided the best stage? That was the knub of the discussion. Lawyers or churchmen? Both had their points to make and as most of those present had first met as members of the Inner Temple the outcome should have been a foregone conclusion. Not so! Robert Wilmot was firmly on the side of the clergy and by the strength of his arguments his friends began to see for the first time where his inclinations were taking him.

'And your opinion, Lawyer Hatton?'

Kit volunteered a wry smile at that. 'If I am the best lawyer you can find then heaven help the law!' They all knew very well that since he had become a member of Her Majesty's circle he had abandoned all attempts to pass his final papers. Why bother? His career was advancing very nicely without such tiresome details. 'Should I have need of legal advice I'd turn to Arden or John here.' Arden Waferer and John Popham took their studies a great deal more seriously than some.

'And though both have a presence which commands attention, neither could outdo a decent clergyman,' Wilmot asserted.

'In a trial they can gain or lose a man his liberty purely by their manner of speech; their actions and personality are invaluable assets. Don't you agree?'

'But a voluble churchman has rescued many a lost cause from the jaws of hell. Where the lawyer fails to save a man and leaves him limping towards the gallows, the man of God stands waiting to turn defeat into a victory.'

'And it's nothing but entertainment for the people. Audience or congregation. All come for a show of some kind.' Henry Noel's laconic tones were neutral. 'This year it has been the only form of entertainment worth seeing. The Queen's illness ruined everything. Nothing new was produced at all.'

'Then it's high time something was! A play! Who's for writing a new play? A contest. We'll write a play each and judge which side produces the better.' Robert Wilmot's freckled face lit up with boisterous enthusiasm.

'Not me. I've no time to be writing plays.'

'Nor me.' Arden Waferer agreed with John

Popham.

'You will, won't you, Kit? And you Henry? Roger? Are you with us? And as for you, my wise and learned stick-in-the-muds, you may play at being the judges you will one day no doubt become. Surely that small task will not gobble up too much of your precious time?'

'Four plays? You expect us to watch four plays and you say it will not take time? But when did the clergy ever know when to finish a sermon?'

'All right then. Not four plays . . .' Robert thought quickly, 'But four separate acts of one play. Each act written by a different actor. It can be done!'

'If we took it from a tale already written so that we know the skeleton of the story we can each take one quarter, and proceed to add meat to the bones. And the judges,' Kit bowed gravely to his two friends, 'could then decide which portion of the carcass tasted best.'

'Agreed. Agreed. But which story do we take?'

The sudden silence which descended over that corner of the hearth caused other customers to eye them curiously for a moment. What were the gentlemen actors plotting now? And would there be parts for real players to show their skills?

'I have it! *Decameron*! Boccaccio's *Decameron*! The tragedy of Tancred's love for his daughter Gismund. That would fall nicely into four pieces, and I have a printed copy by Wynkyn de Worde which will refresh our memories before we begin. And we had better draw lots to see who shall take which part . . .'

At that moment the door of the inn slammed open, letting in a great blast of icy air which carried a frenzied swirl of snowflakes before it into the room. The bulky, well-wrapped figure of a man stood motionless, silhouetted against sober grey of the heavy, afternoon sky.

'Close the door, for God's sake.'

'Hell's teeth! Do you want us all to freeze!'

'Either come or go, but don't just stand there!'

He entered. Ponderously. Menacingly. Many a hand slid round to the hilt of a dagger as the silent stranger stood, feet apart, leaning against the now closed door. What did he want? Every move he made seemed like a threat, even the act of removing the woollen wraps from across his face. Yet all this revealed was an ordinary, everyday person. Except for the scowling anger which was plain enough to be seen even in the dim light of the Boar's Head.

'I look for Christopher Hatton.'

Someone coughed, and a log chose that moment to collapse into the hot ashes in a shower of orange and gold. Otherwise, there was silence. Then Kit rose casually from the oak settle, relaxed and friendly on the outside, but as taut and ready to spring as a baited man-trap on the inside. Not many could beat him in a fight. None, in a fair fight. The man must not know him or he would have been very wary of such a confrontation. Usually Kit's skill with the sword travelled before him and he had rarely been called upon to prove the rumour true. Not since Shea the tinker bled to death, in fact!

'You have found him.'

'Then, sir, I have an argument with you which will not wait.'

'I rather think the weather is too inclement for us to stand in the street. Perhaps you will join us by the fire. And in a drink?'

'This is no idle social chit-chat, sir, and the nature of my quarrel with you is such that you may wish to keep it private.'

Kit was puzzled. He didn't know the man. Of that he was certain. He was in no trouble that he knew of. In debt, certainly. But then again, who wasn't? This didn't look like a debt collector. On the other hand, now that he could study the man's face, he didn't look like a villain either. Just very angry!

'Margery!' Kit called to the ale-wife who was in a back room and quite unaware of the situation in her parlour. 'May we make use of your private room?'

'Of course, deary, but it's not like you to go shouting your intentions to the world.' She bustled in, wiping her hands on her skirts as she spoke. 'Oh . . .' Margery realized that she had mistaken Kit's meaning. Trouble was it? Not a girl!

If she had only known, it was both.

'You have the advantage of me, sir.' Kit raised an eyebrow enquiringly. 'I'm sure we have never met. I rarely forget a face.'

'We have not. But you would appear to have made very close acquaintance with a relative of mine. A very dear relative!' The man's face was turning red with both anger and the warmth after a long ride through ice and snow.

Kit sized him up. Not of the aristocracy, that was certain. A merchant? Possibly. Not wealthy. But not poor either. And not born in London by the sound of him. And how old? Twenty? Twenty-one? Four or five years younger than Kit himself. And a head shorter! Kit placed his right hand firmly on the hilt of his sword.

'You wish to fight before telling me what I am supposed to have done to your family? Or may I first know why I must put my life in jeopardy? And perhaps I should point out to you that I am no novice when it comes to defending myself.' The steely glint in Mister Hatton's eye, and the muscular body now poised to spring, defied the stranger to argue. 'Your name, sir? Before we begin?'

Anger was beginning to be replaced by uneasiness. This man, expensively dressed and exuding confidence, was not the scurvy jackanapes he had been expecting. It might be more prudent to discover what his intentions were . . . Before running him through! Straightening his back, the young man cleared his throat.

'My name, sir, is Hobson. Thomas Hobson of Cambridge. My family own the livery stable there.' He paused, waiting to see if that produced any reaction.

Kit frowned. That name rang a bell! But in what connection . . .? He shook his head. Lord Robert had been in charge of the horses. As Master of the Horse, he and his men had made all the arrangements . . . Hobson? Where had he heard that name?

'I was certainly in Cambridge with Her Majesty in the summer. The first week in August, I believe. But . . .'

'And my sister expects a child in four months' time!' Thomas Hobson's aggression had returned with those words. He took a step forward, anger overcoming caution.

'Hobson! Of course! Nan Hobson! Lovely little Nan! With child?'

Thomas was momentarily taken aback as Christopher Hatton began to laugh. Then, provoked beyond endurance by the conceit of the Queen's favourite he flung himself across the room, arms outstretched and ready to grapple the vile, velvet-clad seducer to the ground. Kit was too quick for him. Gentlemen had never indulged in common fisticuffs and his reflexes stood him in good stead. The blade was unsheathed before either man realized it.

'Hold!' The threat in that one word stopped Tom in his tracks. 'I don't want to hurt you, but make no mistake, I shall if I have to.' The point of the sword was pricking high in Tom's ribs, right on target for his heart if he so much as breathed. 'Back off!'

Tom Hobson held his ground, still glaring at Kit; loathing everything the courtier represented. Such reprobates thought nothing of ruining a girl of respectable family; an innocent girl, well thought of by her friends, whose future as a decent wife and mother had been obliterated by this man's depravity. By his lust. By his prurient fornication. Didn't Mister Hatton know that what was commonplace at Court was considered lewd obscenity in the normal world of ordinary folk? So what was he prepared to do about it? Marry her?

'Impossible.' Kit was no longer laughing. 'I would need permission from the Queen to marry and I can tell you that it would not be forthcoming.' Besides which, he would only want to marry one woman, and that one wouldn't even look at him! As he remembered, Nan was a sweet girl. And a virgin when he met her. Quiet. Pretty. Would she be willing to remain in the background? As his mistress? It was a nice thought. 'Can we talk about this sensibly? If I put up my weapon will you control your emotions long enough for us to find an amicable solution? Please.' Kit turned on the charm. 'Look, you're wet through. Let me have Margery bring us mulled wine and rebuild the fire.'

Smooth talk and a flagon of wine did the trick. Nan could stay in Cambridge until the child was born and then they would think about her moving into London as Kit's . . . er . . . housekeeper. The lodgings in Silver Street were spacious enough for a small family. And now that he had had time to think about it, Kit found the idea rather appealing. Not that he would give up his whores altogether. There was a place for them in every man's life, but if Nan Hobson turned out to be as sympathetic as he remembered it would be pleasant to be indulged by wifely ministrations from time to time. And Mister Hobson was soon won over by a sum of money hastily borrowed by Kit from his curious friends in the other room.

'No trouble,' he assured them grinning. 'A virgin I once knew now sports a swollen belly but believe me, it was no trouble. Just a small loan, to keep her irate brother off my back for a while . . . Come on! Dig deep!'

The erstwhile actor-playwright-lawyers obliged, making ribald jokes at Kit's expense which were as well kept from the ears of Tom Hobson. But hadn't they all been in similiar situations before now? It was at times like these that a man needed friends.

Much later, lying alone in his bed, with shadows creeping from the corners of the room as the fire died down to nothing more than glowing embers, Kit allowed his mind to wander back through time. To that crazy summer of his youth. To Mary Shea. To Meriel. His sister, Dorothy Newport, had raised that child as if she was her own. But love was no barrier to death. In her fourth winter, his lovely little girl, his black-eyed imp, had taken a sudden chill. For two days Meriel had lain, bathed in ice-cold sweat, with her breathing so laboured and painful that Dorothy had cried to watch her. And then death claimed her. Mercifully.

Kit crossed himself in the darkness and prayed. For Mary. For Meriel. For Nan. He needed the Queen's friendship and support if he was ever to win Mary Fytton, and that was his goal; his ultimate aim. And he needed a knighthood to achieve it! But in the meantime, he had a life to live. And a woman to love. God willing. Dear God, don't take Nan as you took Mary . . . Kit's eyes closed. He fell asleep before the prayer was finished.

* * *

What a strange summer it had been. What a strange year! Mary laughed inwardly at the Queen, holding Thomas Heneage's hand as though she never wanted to let it go. Elizabeth was a brilliant actress and had they but known it, put all the players, every one a man, to shame. Heneage was preening himself like a peacock. Revelling in the moment. And what was it all in aid of? It was to show the usual favourites just how much they were out of favour. Mary sidled up to Mister Hatton. How uneasy was he under that suave, polished exterior?

'You have meddled a little too deeply this time. How often do I have to tell you? Stay out of my affairs!' The sly triumph of her smile wasn't even veiled.

Kit could feel his apprehensiveness beginning to show. The Queen had certainly taken note of his insinuations concerning Mary and Henry, Lord Darnley. In February, the mincing deviant had been given permission to visit Scotland and Kit had expected Mary to at least be a little annoyed by the move. That was when he had first had the idea that it had all been some elaborate trap. To his consternation, she had appeared gleeful. Pleased at the move. Now he knew why. The disconcerting news had arrived that Darnley was King of Scotland. Queen Mary had been persuaded to fall madly in love with the boy and had married him! Margaret Lennox had achieved her ambition for her son, against all odds. There was no longer any question of Robert Dudley, Earl of Leicester being sent north, gift-wrapped, to play the rôle of husband, and to his acute dismay. Kit now found himself virtually ignored by the Queen for the part he had played in the affair. What could have come over Mary, Queen of Scots? Darnley was a Catholic, granted. But so were plenty of real men! Elizabeth Tudor had probably had the same thoughts and Kit realized that he would have to tread warily. That the Queen did not think he had actually conspired at this marriage was proved by the fact that he was still at Court, but if she thought for a moment that he would prefer a Catholic Queen on the throne of England . . .! Kit did not relish a life within the confines of the Tower. But by Mistress Fytton's knowing look, the young woman understood far more than she was saying. Yet she was lovely. Fascinating. Bewitching. And untouchable.

Despite Kit's determination to remain dispassionate, Mary caught a glimpse of his continuing devotion in his face.

'You are a fool, sir. Leave well alone.'

'Perhaps you too should have a care.' Where did she get that confidence? She had been lucky this time, but for how long could she hope to manipulate events for her own ends without becoming entangled in the net? She too was a fool if she thought that Robert would ever look at her whilst the Queen remained unmarried. He had noticed, however, that since the death of Kat Ashley, Mistress Mary had seemed to be even closer to the Queen . . . He turned to watch Elizabeth, still holding Tom's hand, laughing happily as he flattered her outrageously, and at the same time trying to coax a smile from Lord Northampton. William was not young and he had long been a friend of the Queen. Since the days when his sister, Queen Katherine Parr had looked after the welfare of the young Princess Elizabeth. He watched as the old man, bent with rheumatism, still played the courtier to his Queen. How did one stay the course? Some seemed to lead charmed lives. Others found themselves locked up, or banished. None, so far in Elizabeth's reign had been beheaded. But that wasn't to say that she wouldn't . . . if the crime warranted it. Kit took a long, hard look at himself, seeing a man who had arrived at Court by sheer good luck, but he recognized that if he was to make the most of his fortune it would have to be by good management. By being prepared to take his chances; by changing sides when necessary. Could he do it? Had he the guts and determination that he saw in Robert? Or was he still, as his uncle had once said, soft? One thing was certain: the man who carried Mary Fytton off to a marriage bed, or indeed any bed, would need to be successful. And therefore ruthless. So why, in heaven's name, did he want her? Thank God for Nan Hobson's plump willingness! And that was a part of his life which was still private. If it hadn't been he could be out of favour with the Queen for ever! He and Robert were supposed to be above such things, and if little Mistress Know-all found out one half the things they sometimes got up to . . .

But his personal life was sorted out and settled. In stark contrast to the insecurity of his public life. Nan had been shy at first, frightened of doing something to offend him; something which would make him angry with her. But she soon realized that the elegant courtier, intimate friend of Elizabeth, Queen of England, was often glad to be rid of the fine trappings and finer manners of the Court; of the wariness necessitated by life in a cut-and-thrust community. His bolt-hole was now a cosy little home, well-managed and relaxing. A place to kick off his boots, pick his nose, and fart to his heart's content. And Nan would still love him! And the baby! An angelic dumpling whose very existence tugged painfully at his heart-strings as it revived memories of his other child. His first-born. But this time it would be different. This time he would be a real father. There to watch her take her first faltering steps; to hear the baby gurgles change magically into words; to behold his rose-bud babe blossom into the full flower of womanhood.

Suddenly conscious of the vacant smile these thoughts had provoked, and realizing that he had once more left himself open to ridicule, Kit braced himself. His Uncle William Saunders *had* been right when he accused him of being soft all those years ago. Too soft for his own good at times! Nan was a good woman, but when it came to a wife . . . How did one make a haughty hell-cat into a wife? He studied Mary's face. Far from being prepared to pour ridicule on him, she had apparently forgotten that he was there as she watched the Queen play cat-and-mouse with Tom Heneage's affections. The young maid's eyes sparkled with amusement. As well they might. Tom had as much hope of a private rendezvous with Elizabeth as he himself had with her servant. A pox take the pair of them! Mistress and maid! Two of a kind! If Mary hadn't been so close to the Queen perhaps he could have resorted to rape? Even as the thought fired the first signs of life for at least ten minutes into his flaccid member he could shrug his shoulders ruefully and sigh. Poor thing! Rose to the occasion every time. When would it learn that the rest of him was simply too flaccid to make the slightest impression on Mistress Fytton, let alone impale her?

'Down, sir!' he silently instructed the wayward organ. 'At least wait until you have her to yourself. You are making a public spectacle of us both.'

It was a regular occurrence but Kit found that sometimes it was almost impossible to contain himself at all. As happened not long afterwards at the christening of the baby Edward Fortunatus in the Chapel Royal at Whitehall.

King Eric of Sweden had sent an unexpected ambassador to England's shores in the cumbersome shape of what appeared to be an overripe fertility goddess. Fecundity in person! His sister, the Princess Cecilia, gave birth within hours of setting foot in Elizabeth's fair land, as if to give it the King's seal of approval. Perhaps a hint of future Swedish princes being born on English soil? The Queen of England had simply smiled demurely at the thought and, with her usual diplomacy, was about to honour the child by becoming his godmother.

Christopher Hatton turned as the fluid glow of candlelight illuminated a darkened staircase leading from the Queen's closet. The Chapel was richly hung with magnificent swathes of cloth-of-gold flanking an immaculately woven arras depicting the Passion of Christ; the altar respendent with gold plate, silver-gilt chalices and crystal bowls. Incense-filled air trembled with the last sweet strains of the choirboys wavering treble as light descended to burst into the body of the church, reflected and magnified a million times by paten and sangrail and by the jewelled raiments of four bishops. Such beauty left Kit quite unmoved. He had eyes for only one, and that one took his breath away. The royal godmother was accompanied by no less that six young virgins, each carrying before her a long, lighted taper. They were dressed in pure white silk. Pearl-sheened. Ethereal. Untouchable.

Untouchable? His unquenchable emblem of manhood didn't seem to think so! Was any other waist so slim and supple? Were any other paps so firm and round? Another neck so white and slender? And the lips! So thoughtlessly sensual! How his friend would love to ruin her for the rôle she played today! How he longed to see her dewy-eyed and eager in his arms; to feel her mouth on his; to feel her naked, virgin flesh . . . Kit stifled a groan, experiencing an anguished torment of the loins which he struggled unsuccessfully to control. Warm. And sticky. Lord, oh Lord! Thank God for ceremonial capes! He shuffled uncomfortably, wrenching his eyes away from the object of his fantasies. Concentrate on something else. Anything else!

Kate Carey carried the screaming infant forward for his part in the day's proceedings and Kit noticed that the Queen had once more managed to show Robert who it was ruled England. The Earl of Leicester had pressed his suit with his mistress a little too earnestly during the summer and quarrelled with Thomas Radcliffe, Earl of Sussex, into the bargain. Sussex had been in favour of the Archduke Charles's suit and Elizabeth had seen fit to put Robert firmly in his place for interference in matters which she insisted did not concern him. Robert and Thomas stood side by side at the font, one holding a basin in which the Queen was to wash her hands, and the other holding a bowl to catch the drips. And neither one saw fit to argue with the arrangements. The power women have over men! Kit glanced at William Parr as he stood beside the other two, towel in hand. Lord Northampton had been married twice already and by the love-sick look on his pouched and sagging face, he was eager to sample the delights of wedlock yet again. Who had tickled the old man's fancy this time? Kit examined the little Swedish girl, another of the Queen's unsullied sirens. Long, white-gold hair cascaded down her back. Enormous eyes of lapis lazuli shone serene and innocent in the flickering light. Fourteen-year-old Helena von Snakenburg had captured an ageing heart.

She had also made an enemy. Mary Fytton was no longer watching the Queen, but stood sulky-mouthed as she scrutinized the girl, and Kit was startled by the expression in those smouldering eyes. It was pure venom!

CHAPTER FIVE

'I have predicted many happenings so accurately that I have amazed even myself. Why, two years ago, whilst travelling abroad, I was overcome with black depression and saw this land laid low by pestilence and destruction. The reason for England's sorry state was revealed to me in a dream; a vision of two queens meeting. So what did I do?' Doctor John Dee paused briefly in mid-flow. Then continuing, he nodded his silver-streaked head as if Mary had replied correctly. 'Yes. I wrote to the Queen and advised her that she should not meet with her cousin, the Queen of Scotland. There will be signs that I speak the truth. Watch for monstrous births, I said. There will be gross deformities manifested throughout the land. And was I right?'

Mary shivered, her skin turning to goose-flesh as he spoke. He looked like everyone's idea of a benevolent uncle, but Blanche Parry's cousin had Celtic blood in his veins and drew knowledge out of thin air. She glanced nervously at Meg Clifford sitting silently beside her. She too seemed to understand such mysteries, as had her old nurse, Elizabeth Fytton. There was a desperate need for these people who lived on the edge of witchcraft;

foretelling futures and warning of disaster. Indeed, that was why she was here. But it frightened her all the same.

'Certainly I was right.' Doctor Dee nodded his head sagely. 'A child was born with two heads and four arms, and a pig in Suffolk was born with human arms instead of trotters. A goat gave birth to a donkey which immediately ate its mother, beginning with the teats which it chewed instead of sucking; and in Shropshire it rained frogs!' As he spoke the mystic slowly removed a cloth of shot silk, covered with strange symbols and trimmed with tassels, from the centre of the table. Underneath was revealed a sphere of solid glass which gave out an insubstantial ebb and flow of rainbow colours in the flickering torchlight, whilst in a corner Dee's pet jay-bird, chained by the leg, suddenly flapped its wings and let out a blood-curdling screech. Mary nearly leapt out of her skin.

'Do you believe me?' His sonorous voice vibrated like a deathknell. 'I only work in the presence of believers.'

Mary nodded her head vigorously. Oh, she believed him all right. It was Meg who had brought her to see him, and her friend had already told her of his powers. What did the future hold for her? That was what she wanted to know. Would the Queen and Robert ever marry? Mary was in the best of company, she knew, in wanting the answer to that seemingly eternal riddle. And yet she understood the problem better than anyone. How could any of the Council, or any of the Queen's courtiers, know of the inner conflict which they, simply by being men, created? How could they, in their vain, egotistical masculinity, ever be able to appreciate that some females could not submit to what they considered to be brutal masculine forces; dared not surrender to aggressive male passions which promised certain pain, and possible death! Yet this very conflict, this unnatural terror, often caused overwhelming guilt. *Normal* women overcame such fears. *Normal* women craved a child to dandle on the knee. And so, as if to prove normality, Elizabeth reacted by being more feminine and flirtatious than ever towards the very men she feared. Desperately more feminine. And Mary herself was torn apart. Hating men and their unquenchable lusts, and at times, hating herself for the transient pleasures she could only find in gentler company. Was there no escape from this vicious, soul-destroying circle? Could anyone free her? Turn her into an ordinary, loving woman? Only one man in the whole world caused her heart to beat faster, and her breath to catch in her throat. But it was not through love. It was through fear. She had recognized the harsh scent of a rutting male. In the rumpled linens of the Queen's bed. As though he had marked his territory. Like a wild beast . . .

'We are beginning to see.' John Dee was visibly relaxed, arms resting motionless on either side of the sphere and eyelids drooping as he peered into its magical centre; into another world. Into the future. Strange and pleasantly sweetish odours filled the room, carried on pale spirals of smoke emanating from the crucible, pervading the atmosphere with tranquillity and calm. Inducing a kind of trance in the three occupants.

Mary felt the corners of the room soften and become rounded. Almost as though it was taking on the shape of the object in the middle of the table. A cradle. A haven from the cruel world. A womb. Warm and dark and comforting. She was no longer afraid. For hours the doctor had pored over his charts, divining all the aspects at the time of her birth; aligning heavenly bodies; deciphering portents. What would he find?

'You think a woman holds the key to your fate. But this is not so. I see a dagger. And a sword. A gipsy . . . Dead. And a sailor. Also dead by the same sword. The name on both men's lips . . . Mary! Turn to the victor . . . Ah . . . A child. An open hearth . . . The sword is sheathed . . . Too late . . .'

A sailor? Mary shook her head. She knew no common sailors and neither did she want to. But a gipsy? There were those who likened Robert Dudley to the Romanies, on account of his swarthy complexion and dark, flashing eyes . . . Dead? Killed by the sword? Not King of England? But a child? What did he mean by a child? Whose child? Not Mary Fytton's. That was certain!

'What does it all mean?' she whispered into Meg's ear, surprised to find her friend twisting the ring on her finger nervously and biting at her lower lip.

'Too late? Too late for what? What did you see?' Meg's voice in the stillness startled the doctor.

The glazed look was beginning to leave his eyes as he collected his wits together. He could never tell all that he had just witnessed. It was horrible. A nightmare. Vile and terrifying murder. Sometimes John Dee wondered why he didn't stick to his globe of the world and his charts of the trade routes. He was on much firmer ground expounding his theories of the north-east passage, an as yet undiscovered stretch of water which would lead men straight to China. Or the great southern continent which he had persuaded himself sat waiting for Englishmen to plunder. *Terra Australis*! And yet there was a fascination which was hard to ignore in the study of alchemy and astrology. Where did such visions come from? Would these things come to pass?

Mistress Mary had a puzzled look which indicated that she hadn't understood a word of what he had said. Which was just as well. But

Meg Clifford was a different matter. She had a feeling for these things, as he did himself, though not so pronounced. And he should warn her. Warn her not to get too involved with the Queen's young maid!

'When the time comes,' he looked sternly at Meg, 'You must come to me and I will again look into the glass. Do nothing without my word.' His voice was heavy and ominous. 'One wound you will heal . . .' His words trailed into silence. She understood the unspoken rule. Only reveal the good. The evil must remain inside him. His burden. His penance for meddling in such things.

'And my future?' Mary could feel strange undercurrents.

'You will be honoured by the highest in the land. The highest. But you must excuse me. I must show my Monas to Cecil who, I believe, is interested in the mystical symbols and magic numbers which it contains.' Doctor Dee had been brought to the Queen's notice by his cousin Blanche, and after casting Her Majesty's horoscope for the coronation had been promised a sinecure. He had awaited the fulfilment of this promise by travelling abroad and now he deemed the time to be right for collecting his dues. His numerous contacts in Europe would be of interest to both the Queen and her Secretary of State. As were his symbols, signs and numbers. Spying and setting up codes could bring their own rewards! With luck he would one day be a man of substance. Unless the crystal continued to show him sights which made his blood run cold. In which case he would shortly be nothing more than a gibbering wreck.

In the Great Hall the festivities were continuing. The slim figure of the Queen, fetchingly dressed in a kirtle of gold shot with green, and matching green velvet gown, twisted and twirled to the music with all the energy of a new-born lamb. And Robert partnered her to perfection in yellow satin trimmed with sable. Mary watched the couple, so well matched for elegance and wit; for style, and dress. Yet never to be paired as mates. Of that she was now assured. During the autumn, Robert had been restored to full favours by Elizabeth and Mary had had the uneasy feeling that something was undermining her own secret relationship with the Queen. Nothing had been said. But there had been an undercurrent of change. Vague and unformed. Nothing definite. Simply a feeling. An intuition. Resulting in her visit to Doctor Dee. And there she had found reassurance. Amongst the company dancing she saw the Princess Cecilia and her husband and several of their entourage. The Queen had made a great fuss of them when they first arrived but it was plain to see that they were outstaying their welcome. Despite the fact that the Queen had been more than generous in paying their expenses they had managed to become indebted to merchants all over the town. So far as Mary was concerned, the sooner they boarded their vessel to return whence they came, the better. She could not stand those simpering Swedish maids. Fair and fragile, they set her teeth on edge. It was since they had arrived that the Queen had been paying more attention to Robert. And not through guilt. Or was it? There was a niggling doubt at the back of Mistress Fytton's mind, and try though she might she could not dismiss it.

Ambrosc Dudlcy and thc ncw Lady Warwick were also in the company this New Year's Eve. Little Anne Russell had made an excellent match, and by the love-look on her face it was an affair of the heart too. Mary shuddered. The fires at either end of this huge room did nothing to eliminate the winter draughts. What did Anne feel like now that she was wed? Had it hurt? If it had then she obviously enjoyed pain. She never took her eyes from her husband. After the magnificence of the christening in September, the Chapel Royal had again been decked out in its finery for the November wedding. Robert had given the bride away and Mary had thought at the time that she had never seen him look so regal. Royal purple and gold. It suited him perfectly. And then at the tournament held to celebrate the event he had been the only man worth watching. Both Mary and the Queen had watched him intently. Of course, Hatton had poked his nose in as he did at every opportunity, asking to wear her favour; bowing and scraping to her behind the Queen's back. An impoverished country squire! A shadow fell across her as she leaned against the tapestried wall. Lordy! Here he was again. Would she never be rid of him?

'Mistress.' Kit saw the impatience on her face as he bowed his greeting. And that was before he had even spoken! Why? What in the world had the woman got against him?

'May I be so bold as to introduce Lord President of Connaught and Thomond, here in company with the Earl of Ormonde, both recently arrived on business from Ireland.'

Mary took stock of the stranger. She had noticed the earl, tall, dark and extremely handsome as he was. Black Tom. One of the Queen's lesser favourites, but a favourite, nonetheless. This man, however, had golden hair. Gold with a glint of burnished bronze. And dark blue eyes. So dark that they were almost violet in colour. They eyed each other curiously.

'Mistress, may I introduce Sir Edward Fytton.'

Mary froze in mid-curtsey.

'Sir, this is one of the Queen's young maids, Mary Fytton.'

Sir Edward shook his head. 'Mary seems to be a common name amongst the Fyttons. My mother is Mary, as is my sister. And my daughter Mary is barely three years old. But I was not aware that any of my kin was at present waiting on Her Majesty.'

'I fear, sir, that you were misled.' Mary shot Kit a withering glance. 'I have never been to Ireland.'

At this the two men exchanged smiles. Had she said something amusing?

'My present post is in that country, certainly, as Treasurer of Ireland, but my birthplace and my true home is here in England. Cheshire, to be exact. Gawsworth Hall.'

Even in the shadows of the hall they could see that the information had startled her. Or frightened her.

'You know it?'

'I know of it, sir, though I have never been there.'

Damn Kit Hatton to hell! What should she do? Lie? She couldn't tell the truth and that was certain!

'Then you are kin? Though distant perhaps . . .' Edward Fytton's curiosity was aroused. She was a lovely-looking woman. Quite beautiful enough to be a Fytton. No wonder Mister Hatton was so smitten with her. If he himself had been younger . . . But then again, there was his wife Anne, bedmate for nearly twenty-seven years. And eleven children, with another on the way!

Mary took a deep breath. 'Not kin, sir. I'm afraid the connection is much slighter. I am a poor orphan and my origins are as much a mystery to me as they are to others. But my nurse was a woman who I believe did once live at Gawsworth Hall. Elizabeth Fytton. She was once maid to Anne Boleyn, and a good friend of that tragic queen. For this reason Her Majesty has seen fit to look kindly on me and has given me all the advantages of a place amongst her ladies. Mistress Fytton lives far away in retirement now and since she brought me to Court I have not set eyes on her.' Mary refrained from telling the two men of the visits to the old witch made by Meg Clifford. The Queen did not want anyone spying into the affair of Elizabeth Fytton and her foundling child. Or it would be the worse for Mary.

'Elizabeth? Maid to Anne Boleyn? That would be my father's sister. Disgraced the family name by running off with one of our numerous cousins and ruining her chances of a fine marriage. And then the lad she ran off with had the misfortune to lose his head with Queen Anne.'

'Shh!' Mary was quick to hush him. It was not wise to talk of Elizabeth Tudor's mother in connection with her supposed lovers. There were enough Catholics around willing to call the Queen a bastard as it was! Probably Kit Hatton was one of them! Was that his game? Did he still have hopes of Mary, Queen of

Scots?

'Hmmmph! Well, yes.' Edward realized his mistake. Best leave the subject alone. He had no wish to be on the wrong side of Her Majesty's temper. A difficult enough job at the best of times. All over Black Tom one minute, and then flinging herself at Robert Dudley like a girl in the first bloom of love. God preserve England from petticoats! He thought this an excellent moment to take his leave and let these two young people sort out their problems in their own way.

The minute he was out of earshot Mary turned on Kit.

'Are you completely witless, sir?' Will you not give up until the world has seen the last of me? By all that is holy, sir, what do you hope to gain?' She was shaking with fury. Panicked out of her usual calm assurance.

Kit took her arm as those closest to them began to stare. 'Perhaps we had better go elsewhere.'

In her anger Mary allowed herself to be led out to a small cosy away from the crowds and festivities. She was in no mood to watch others dance, free from worry. What was happening to her life all of a sudden? Robert was going all out to win the Queen, and the Queen only had eyes for Robert. That Swedish von Snakenburg was forever on a cushion at Elizabeth's feet these days! And now Hatton was stirring up trouble for her as only he could.

In the privacy of the little room, set out with stools and a table for gaming, Mary rounded on her tormentor.

'You play dangerous games, but make no mistake about it! If you destroy me I shall drag you down with me. There are things about this world which you will never understand. The world is full of evil which no amount of good will ever undo. And I hate you enough to make an end of you, Mister Hatton.'

Kit couldn't doubt it. With her arms supporting her she leaned across the intervening table, cheeks flushed and eyes aglow with fervour. What a waste of passion! A pulse spot throbbed steadily on her slender neck. Make an end of him would she? He'd have to see about that! Almost stealthily he began to move towards her round the table. The girl lived in a dream world, elevating herself to some imagined position of importance. Who but Kit Hatton cared a damn about her true identity? It could hardly be the subject of national security she fancied. It was probably the only way the poor child could justify her existence. Surrounding herself with an aura of mystery. Having a reason to give herself airs. Well! It was time to put an end to such nonsense!

Before Mary had time to realize what was happening he had her in his grasp; pinning her arms to her sides as his mouth crushed hers with a violent, bruising kiss. Physically, she knew herself defenceless against the steely, muscular strength of this courtier. Only last month she had watched as he effortlessly unseated half the Court in the joust at Anne Russell's wedding. But there were other ways of cooling a man's ardour! She ceased her struggles and for a moment he thought he had overcome her resistance. The fierce pressure of his lips on hers became less forceful; more sensuous; his tongue finding its way inquisitively between her teeth; his hands relaxing their grip to allow his arms to embrace her. Holding her body close. Feeling the warmth. The feminine curves.

Mary struggled desperately with the instinct to fight him off; with the revulsion which made her sick to her stomach. The last time a man had been as close as this . . . She remembered the vile beast straddling her back as she lay on the earthen floor of the barn . . . The tearing agony . . . Don't! Don't think about it. But now she could feel him hard against her belly through the silks and petticoats . . . That cruel instrument of torture . . .

Kit had not expected such a quick capitulation, but it was only a matter of seconds before he realized that there was no active response to his caresses either. Puzzled and disappointed, he gazed into the darkest pair of eyes since Mary Shea. Then Mistress Fytton threw back her head and laughed. On and on. She laughed until tears ran down her face; as though she had never witnessed anything so funny in her life. Kit began to feel embarrassed. What was so funny? The way he kissed? What? The more Mary laughed the more inadequate he felt. His pisser drooped. Then shrivelled. Until it was smaller and more useless than a wick without tallow.

'What is it?' Kit's discomfort was turning to anger. 'What in God's name is there to laugh about?'

Mary's dark eyes glinted slyly. 'Today Doctor Dee foretold some of the future, using charts and symbols. And a magic glass.' The taunting peals of laughter rang out again. 'No mention of a humble squire! No pretty courtier dancing to the Queen's tune . . . My future lies with the highest in the land. It is written in the stars!'

'John Dee?' Kit crossed himself automatically, an old and trusted Latin prayer on his lips.

'Ha!' Mary pounced. 'Papist!' She spat the word in his face, eyes narrowed wickedly. 'Does your mistress know? Shall I tell her? Or Lord Robert?' The Earl of Leicester was so far removed from Kit's religious beliefs as to be a Puritan.

Motionless, they stared at each other, the air round them charged with open hostility. Now she had a weapon. And a shield! Mister Hatton would have to mind his manners from now on or he would find himself back in obscurity, or worse, before he could blink. And they both knew it. Mary's cunning smile spelt victory as she sidled past him to the door. Let the upstart make one false move. Just one!

But Mary was not to have it all her own way on that New Year's Eve, 1565. On returning to the hall she found that the dancing was over, and that the Queen had retired with the Earl of Leicester, taking for company Elin von Snakenburg, Lord Northampton making a fourth in the games of Primero or Gleek. Damn Kit Hatton to hell! Mary paced nervously for hours but she was not called. William Parr eventually left the Queen's private rooms with the blondhaired Swede on his arm. Robert did not emerge till morning.

Imagination tormented her. Had they simply played cards? Or made love? Even Mary didn't dare ask. Like the rest of the Court she could only wait. And wonder.

If there were any expecting marriage to be the outcome of these events, it was as well they didn't hold their breath. The moment passed and Robert was again left brooding on what he had to do to become king. In the spring the Court at last waved a thankful farewell to the Princess Cecilia and her party. Or most of it! Little Elin turned those limpid blue eyes on Elizabeth Tudor and begged to stay in the land she had come to love in so short a time. Amongst the people she had learnt to love. To

Mary's disgust the child was made Gentlewoman of the Bedchamber, constantly in the company of the Queen, and determined to insinuate herself into Elizabeth's affections.

Whether it was these developments, or whether it was simply natural, mutual dislike, Mary was unsure, but Robert seemed to be quarrelling with everyone in sight. A confrontation with Sussex over Ireland had left a strained atmosphere, and in addition, he had been heard arguing with Thomas Howard over something of nothing. Not that that was anything new! Tom had never seen eye to eye with Robert in the matter of what he thought to be the over-familiarity of the Queen's Master of the Horse with Her Majesty. In fact he had once offered to alter the shape of Robert's face in the middle of a tennis match if he failed to show more respect to his monarch. Tom Howard's mediocrity was shown nothing more than contempt, but as Duke of Norfolk, despite his Catholic sympathies, his name carried considerable weight in England, and this rankled. So far as Robert was concerned, the man, duke or not, was an interfering, insufferable bore.

There was news too which put the Queen out of sorts. In June it was learned that Mary, Queen of Scots had given birth to a boy. Others were not so dismayed. At last, a possible future King! If Elizabeth failed to produce an heir . . . Especially if the Protestant

Earls of Scotland could gain control of the boy . . . Kit Hatton was quick to send his congratulations. As was Lord Robert. Loyalty to Elizabeth did not insist on discourtesy to her cousin. And it was certainly beginning to look as though Elizabeth would die without issue. Possibly without ever marrying!

One direct result of this news was that Mary Fytton was once more in close attendance on the Queen. Her Majesty's headaches had returned with a vengeance and no one, she declared, could soothe them away like Mary. The summer progress found them at Oxford, and the Queen settled in her palace of Woodstock for a short season.

The orations were over and the Queen had withdrawn. At last Robert could relax from his duties, and the evening found him, in company with Kit Hatton, mulling over the oratories and speeches of the previous days.

'And what did you think of the play?' Robert motioned his servant to refill the cups.

'Well done, and even better dedicated!' Kit grinned, raising his drink in tribute. Robert was highly thought of in literary circles these days and Tom Nunce had done the right thing in choosing the earl as his patron. His Latin play, *Octavia* had honoured Robert's name, spelling out the thanks of numerous scholars who were indebted to him for his interest in their efforts.

'But I'll have them writing every mortal

thing in English before I'm done! So even men of little learning can learn to love our language. And talking of love . . .' Robert winked at his drinking companion. 'You were there when I bestowed the honorary degree on John Sheffield? Did you notice his wife?'

Kit shook his head.

Robert whistled appreciatively. 'Now I wouldn't say no to a romp with young Douglass Howard, given half a chance.'

'And is she? The type, I mean?' Kit's eyes gleamed mischief over the brimming cup of ruby wine.

'What Howard isn't? Remember Katherine? And Anne Boleyn, by all accounts. She too was a Howard on her mother's side.'

'The trait hasn't rubbed off onto our Queen though. I should think you would have better luck with almost anyone. Though of course, Douglass is married.'

'I wasn't thinking of marrying her.' Robert chuckled, biting into a thick wedge of rabbit pie. 'I may be a fool but I still have hopes of Elizabeth. I've been as close as . . . Well, as close as any man could be . . .' He wiped a dribble of gravy from his beard, '. . . but she's too independent for a woman, damn her! I'll tell you one thing though; if she marries anyone at all it will be Robert Dudley, Earl of Leicester. The others are mere politics, or in some cases, simply used to play on my jealousy. But all that doesn't stop me wanting a young and eager woman from time to time. And I don't mean a casual whore. I mean a woman. Like your Nan, perhaps. Someone to go home to at night, knowing that there will always be a welcome.'

'I doubt that Douglass Howard would be as compliant as Nan. Ladies seldom are. But Nan expects so little from life, or from me for that matter, that it is the easiest thing in the world to please her. She's soft and warm, but despite her gentleness, she is as willing in bed as any whore. It's her way of being sure I always return.'

'Will you, do you think?' Robert knew that he would still be trying to get into Elizabeth Tudor's bed when she was a toothless old hag. But would he if she were not Queen?

Kit was under no illusions about himself. 'I shouldn't think so. I'm determined to be successful at Court, and part of that ambition involves that black-eyed bitch Mary. Nan has her uses at the moment, but who knows what the future may hold in store.' Kit drained his cup once more. 'But my baby! Now that is different. You must see her one day. She is a real beauty and with luck I shall find her a place at Court one of these days.'

Robert couldn't help but see the pride which lit up his friend's face at the mention of his daughter. What must it be like to have a child? Would he ever find out? But first he needed a woman!

'I shall write her a note. She had that look . . . You know, when a woman gives an invitation with a single glance . . .'

'Be careful of her husband then. Or you may get more than you bargained for. And if it reached Elizabeth's ears . . . Well, rather you than me.' At least there was no problem with Nan. She was not likely to go shouting his business about the town in case she found herself out on her arse.

'Husbands; fathers; erstwhile lovers. Haven't we dealt with them all before now? If they become too inquisitive, or too tetchy about the affair . . .' That lop-sided grin, which the ladies seemed to find so adorable, had sinister undertones. But Kit understood. There were few questions asked if the suspect held a high enough position. And few were higher than Robert.

Amongst those few, however, were the members of the Royal Houses, and the following February news arrived in London which was received in stunned silence by all. Henry, Lord Darnley, was dead. Murdered! Robert's words came back to Kit.

'Tetchy husbands? Haven't we dealt with them all before now?'

It had surprised Kit that Mary, with her reputation for beauty and vivacity, had agreed to wed the girlish Darnley in the first place. But murder! And so public! Had she really been so stupid as to think she could get away with it? Dear Lord! The woman must be a half-wit. Gone forever was the plan to see her on the throne of England. There was no possible way in which she could redeem herself. The Catholic cause was lost.

Robert, who had been keeping a weather eye on the situation north of the border, in consideration of Mary, Queen of Scots having borne a son, didn't hesitate. His brother was immediately despatched to make overtures to Edward Seymour, Earl of Hertford, whilst Robert himself approached the Earl's mother, Anne, Duchess of Somerset. Katherine Grey, the real reason for these manoeuvres, was still living separately from her husband at the Queen's command. But if Elizabeth suddenly took ill and died . . . It was as well to declare your friendships well in advance!

Kit kept his own council on the happenings in Scotland and did his level best to ignore the gleeful insinuations of Mary Fytton. Besides which, there was little anyone could do for the foolish Queen whilst she was under strict guard, and imprisoned by her own people. But within a year the tangled mess surrounding the succession to the English throne had tied itself in another knot. On a frosty January morning, Lady Katherine Grey, who had long been losing the will to live, died. Reduced almost to a skeleton by the endless grief of her young life; by the enforced and cruel separation from the handsome husband she had married for love against the Queen's wishes, she silently passed into a world more forgiving of human frailty.

And in the spring, Mary, Queen of Scots, gave her captors the slip and took refuge in a land *she* hoped would be more forgiving. England!

* * *

Belvoir Castle dominated the village and surrounding countryside, perched high, as it was, on an elevated spur above thickly wooded slopes. Though it had been previously allowed to fall into a dismal state of repair, the Earl of Rutland had dipped into his pocket sufficiently deep enough to feel the place worthy of a visit from his Queen. The magnificent views over the Leicestershire Wolds were deserving of the visit on their own. At least, so Robert Dudley thought.

'Manners seems to have done himself proud.' Robert and Kit rode side by side on the broad and winding pathway. Dense, deciduous woodlands opened, here and there, into light-dappled glades of soft, tufted grass, or romantic, fern-shaded hollows. 'Isn't it just the place for a summer tryst?'

'Summer tryst?' Kit eyed his travelling companion curiously. What was Robert up to now?

'I may as well tell you. In case I need help.

You know! A stolen hour here. A few snatched minutes there. Someone has to keep the Queen fully occupied. And the lady's husband unsuspecting!'

Kit shook his head, pretending an attack of offended morals.

'And whilst I am covering your tracks, nerves stretched to breaking, you will be enjoying a rollicking good time with another man's wife! Shame on you, sir! Have you no decency?'

'None whatsoever. No more than you, in fact!' A deep-throated chuckle soon became a full and open laugh as Robert remembered some of the more recent nights of debauchery, during which, Mister Hatton had been as much in evidence as any. 'And you know that I'd do the same for you. You only have to ask.'

'And you know that it is most unlikely that I ever will. You can keep your ladies of the Court. They hold little attraction for me, I'm quite content to keep on the right side of the Queen and snuggle up to Nan when the mood takes me.'

'Mary is out of favour then?'

'Very much out of favour. I don't know what I saw in her in the first place! She is nothing but a vain, ill-mannered temptress. Leading men on with her come-hither looks. And then laughing in their faces when nature makes the results of her teasing prominent. I can take such treatment from the Queen as she does not have the same painful physical effect on my poor, perplexed member. In Mary's company he's all attention one minute and grovelling in abject misery the next. No. You take the so-called ladies. I'll take the whores. At least they finish what they promise!'

Although Kit tried to modulate his tone it didn't take a genius to see that his monumental failure with that one woman was a major source of irritation to him. Her name was so much gall and wormwood on his tongue that he spat it out in an effort to be rid of it.

'If you take my advice, you'll forget her.' Robert could concede that the woman was attractive, but hardly worth all the trouble Kit had gone to. 'But you're wrong to condemn all ladies for the faults of one. Unless I have completely misread the signs the one who waits for me is more than willing. And probably awaits my coming right at this moment. In fact it might be better if she was forewarned of our arrival so that she can compose herself and not give our little game away in her excitement.'

Kit couldn't help smiling. Robert was not being conceited, though to a stranger it might well have sounded so. He was already three steps ahead in the game of hide-and-seek which was about to commence, covering tracks which had not yet been laid and guarding against errors which had not yet been made.

'Ride ahead, will you? Make sure that

everything is ready for Elizabeth. I shall accompany her with the rest of the party.'

'So! My duties begin right here!' Kit shrugged his shoulders in resignation and slapped his horse's rump. A good-natured laugh as he rode away assured Robert that he was in no way averse to the involvement.

The clatter of hooves on the cobbles brought a stablehand running to fetch him to the mounting-block, and had a manservant waiting at the door of the castle. They also brought the distinct rustle of petticoats and a delicious feminine fragrance. The heady scent of honeysuckle at evening. Wild and rambling, but in close proximity, cloying. Almost suffocating.

Before him stood that frivolous scatterbrain; that pretty and eager piece of nonsense, Douglass Howard.

* * *

The twilight clarity of Midsummer's Eve glittered with a hundred silver stars above the trees which stood, shoulder, to shoulder, arms outstretched, covering the woodland dells with a deep-green mantle of privacy. An owl hooted forlornly. The vole impaled upon his talons, tail still twitching in death, would have suited him better had it been a rat. Or a young rabbit. Still, it would serve as an entrée. The sharp, curved beak tore into soft, grey-brown fur and one tiny drop of blood spilled down from the leafy canopy to hang suspended from a wisp of grass. A ruby pendant, shining briefly in the glow-worm's phosphorescence.

Douglass Howard saw no cruel predator. Nor airy victim caught in a deadly situation. Nor did she smell death in the thrilling, secretive air of her romantic fairyland; in the Utopia of her lover's arms. She noticed only the unique scent of their lovemaking; a blend of breath and sweat and the compelling, irresistible odour of silken fluids produced at the climax of their passion. She kissed the strength of his shoulder, and the black hair curling darkly across his chest. She kissed the smooth expanse of abdomen, her warm, pointed tongue delicately exploring that minute pit, nature's regular blemish, his navel. And then, with reverence, she kissed that precious organ of delight, her tumbled hair caressing his naked flesh as she bowed her head to perform this sacred ritual; this obsequious homage.

Robert Dudley groaned as he felt his body begin to respond to the delightful feelings the woman evoked.

'Again? So soon?'

'I love you. I love you. I love you.' Her hands continued the caresses her mouth had started. 'I never want to let you go. So I shall make you stay. For a little longer. Who knows when we shall meet like this again? And I want you now as I shall always want you. Like this.' Poised momentarily above him, she spread her legs and lowered herself very, very slowly into position. Robert groaned again as his defenceless body shook with another paroxysm of ecstasy.

'Do you love me?' Douglass asked the inevitable question.

Despite his physical turmoil, Robert was a long way from losing his head, but the passion of the kiss he gave her then was no play-act.

'If I had the power, I should make this moment last a lifetime. This hour we have shared, this hour of love, would be as endless as the night I would create. Dawn would never be allowed to creep silently between the trees to point accusing fingers; to cast shadows across such a perfect union.'

'Oh, Robert . . . If only . . .'

'Hush now. It won't be the last time. I promise. If we can find a way once, then we can find a way again. But only if it is kept secret. You have a husband. And truth to tell, I would find myself in the worst possible trouble with Elizabeth if she ever found out.'

That was certainly a fact, and Robert wanted no such problems whilst there was still the slightest chance of the Queen ever taking him as a husband. On the other hand, Douglass was a hot and very willing woman when it came to a frolic. And it was a pity to waste a meal served to him so appetizingly, on a plate.

'It isn't just the secrecy which adds the spice? You do love me, don't you?'

'Haven't I said so?' He hadn't, but Douglass let it pass. Now, the ardour beginning to cool with her predictable questions, sanity once more raised its head. It was time to go.

'Kit will be blessing us if we don't make an appearance soon. Or at least, if I don't.'

Douglass had pleaded a headache and asked the Queen's permission to retire early. If anyone discovered that she was not in her room she could always say that she had stepped outside, thinking that the fresh air might help her. Robert, on the other hand, had begged leave to attend to some business with the horses. Bay Star had needed a dressing under her belly and it was suspected that one of the Queen's mounts was suffering from the farcy, a painful infection which produced clusters of boils within the nose. He had paid a brief visit to the stables and given instructions before continuing to keep his rendezvous with Douglass, but he would have to call again to make sure his orders had been carried out before he rejoined the house-party.

The lovers parted company in the shadows of a tall hedge at the borders of the formal gardens and Douglass made her way through the dimly lit passages of the servants' quarters to the room she shared with John Sheffield. There she hugged herself in the excitement of remembered thrills and read once more the beautiful love-letter, written in his own hand, by which means Robert had arranged this first and very satisfying assignation. She would carry it with her everywhere, next to her heart. It was the only item she possessed which had been his. A physical reminder of one fleeting hour of perfect happiness.

* * *

John Sheffield's anger had become somewhat diluted with trepidation after a frustrating week in London, where he had hoped to confront none other than the great Earl of Leicester. The very man who had, only a couple of years previously, invested him with an honorary degree. Bitterness and suspicion now ruined the remembered pride of that occasion as he constantly fingered the crumpled edges of a certain *billet-doux.* The man was avoiding him. On purpose. Mister Sheffield had kept on his toes, bright and alert; the first to arrive in the Queen's corridor each morning and the last to leave each night, his beady eyes raking over everyone entering, whether they had business with the Queen or not. Searching continuously for that one face.

But Lord Robert was busy, Kit Hatton assured the impatient cuckold. Problems between the Queen of Scots and her Protestant Lords. A ticklish business.

Delegated to Thomas Howard and Tom Radcliffe, neither of them trusted friends of the Earl of Leicester. Therefore it was obvious, wasn't it, that Robert must be careful to know what their stand in the matter would be? And after all, where this other affair was concerned . . . Well, a mistake could not be ruled out. Could it? Kit did his best to cool the irate Lord Sheffield down, as Robert had asked, and, with his easy-going, friendly manner, was succeeding admirably.

Robert's unavailability was noticed in other quarters too. Mary Fytton liked to know the movements of the Queen's lover and this overzealous display of discretion puzzled her. Something was going on. She could sense it. But what? That conceited ne'er-do-well Mister Hatton infuriated her by treating her like an interfering child. Hell take the man! Wasn't he supposed to be in love with her? Why was he covering up? What trouble was Robert in this time? Perhaps Meg would know.

Lady Strange was sitting alone in a small sunlit cosy, her head bent industriously as she scribbled strange signs and symbols onto a square of parchment. Such nonsense meant nothing to Mary and she moved casually to the casement and into the warmth of the sun, not speaking. Biding her time. Choosing her words. Meg had odd dealings with Robert occasionally, she knew. Acting as a go-between with Doctor Dee.

'How will they resolve the problem of the Scots Queen do you think? Will the Papist turn? For the throne of England?'

Meg paused in her writing, her bland features fashioned into an imperturbable smile.

'I doubt she'll live to mount the throne. Even supposing that she wants it.'

'Of course she wants it!' Mary looked scornfully at her friend. How could anyone not want it? She shook her head. Meg lived in a dream world sometimes.

'But what do you mean, if she lives? Shc isn't ill, is she? I haven't heard that she is.'

'Not ill. Oh, no. Frightened of being ill though.' Meg's expression never changed. 'Very frightened. So I believe. But she has friends in high places. Even in her cousin's Court. And if one resorts to violence another will come to her rescue, never fear.'

Mary couldn't have cared less. Unless it involved Robert. Did it? Was that what Meg's knowing smile was about?

'Friends?'

'Well, one friend, at least.' Meg had the knack of saying a lot with very few words. She bent her head again to read those she had just finished writing. Her next comment was scarcely audible. 'But he should occasionally look over his shoulder or he may be brought low himself by his enemy.'

Mary felt her back stiffen and the hairs raise

themselves on the back of her neck. There were always enemies at Court . . . But Robert was distracted by the problem of Scottish politics . . . Perhaps he wouldn't realize . . . Damn Kit Hatton. He knew the whole story, she was sure. But if Robert had trusted the Queen's prancing partner to protect him from . . . From what?

'Tell me, Meg. Tell me all you know.'

'That's little enough.' Meg's soft voice would not be hurried. 'Only that Lord Sheffield, being slightly drunk in the Bull down in Bishopsgate Street the other night, was overheard to describe the gory details of a certain person's death, should they meet in some dark alleyway. He was not too drunk to imagine that the deed could be accomplished in broad daylight, however!'

'But why? What is his quarrel?' Mary frowned. Robert had nothing in common with John Sheffield. That she was aware of, at any rate. Money? Land? It had to be something of that nature then.

Meg shrugged her shoulders. 'I can only tell you what was repeated to me. Threats by night, and pestering Mister Hatton every minute of the day. He's angry about something. That's certain. And getting angrier by the hour. There will be trouble sooner or later, mark my words.'

Mary shuddered despite the sun on her shoulders. Meg Clifford had an eerie voice. So quiet that she seemed to whisper, and yet her words carried with all the clarity of a bell. And she knew things. Strange things. Strange by nature as well as name. If Meg forecast trouble, then trouble there would be.

'You'll excuse me?' Meg rose silently from the seat, rolling her parchment carefully and secreting it into the hidden pocket of her petticoats. She had said enough. Having known Mary since she arrived at Court, a young, awkward colt of a girl, she had watched her develop into one of the true beauties of Queen Elizabeth's retinue. Beautiful but . . . unstable? Was that the word she was searching for? Unbalanced? And very close to Her Majesty. Too close for many to divulge their most intimate secrets. It was as well if the Queen did not know quite everything which went on in her Court!

The dull click of the wooded door-latch in the stillness of the room told Mary that she was alone with her thoughts as bubbles of hate began to ferment inside her. She recognized the signs. Nervous excitement would be followed by cold, contained anger. Then she would concentrate. Hard. And she would plan. Had anyone been able to observe the young woman as she sat there, drenched in an aura of golden light, her delicately modelled porcelain features perfectly composed, they would have been hard pressed to read her mind. Ideas chased themselves around her brain like dogs after cats after birds after gnats. Could she gain anything from the situation? Bring the Queen's displeasure down on Robert again? But how? How could it be done? Get rid of John Sheffield, perhaps?

Her mind cleared. As it had that time when she had accompanied Meg to Cumnor Place . . . She had only been a child then, but old enough to understand that Robert was only waiting for his sick wife to die in order that he might marry the Queen. And there had been no doubt that the woman was going to die. She had been mortally ill. How easy it had been to say that she had forgotten a glove . . . How still and empty the house when she left. And Amy, so peaceful at the foot of the stairs. Robert had escaped blame, but the event had caused suspicion and rumour to run high. Elizabeth was no fool and had realized at once that marriage to her handsome courtier was now out of the question. Behaving like a radiant bride until the sudden death of Amy Robsart had shocked her to her senses. It had been the very douce of icy water she had needed.

And still, all these years later, Robert was still embraced by Her Majesty the Queen in the privacy of her private chambers. Would she ever see him as he really was? Arrogant. Avaricious. With his spies and silent band of henchmen who only awaited his command. They were well paid for their work, she knew. And Meg, with her potions and simples!

Called upon many a time to . . . er . . . help. Potion or poison? Who could tell? In fact, that was the answer! A certain way to be rid of Lord Sheffield! Meg would provide the means . . . A lie would suffice to procure the ratsbane. Find the name of the man's lodging-house from another source and deduce whether his landlady could be bribed. Or frightened!

The blood was beginning to zing through her veins. Intoxicating. Exhilarating. The reasons for the plan were being chased into second place by sheer blood-lust. The need to control. The need for power. Glancing through the window Mary could see Elizabeth strolling through the ornamental gardens with that prurient milksop, Hatton. There too, she had power. The more Hatton fawned and slobbered, the more the Queen would despise him for it. Oh, she might give him some small reward, as she might give a titbit to her favourite horse, but she would despise him all the same for trying to buy her with his body. With his masculinity. Mary couldn't help chuckling to herself. If only those strutting peacocks realized how ludicrous they were! And how thrilling to be instrumental in ridding the world of one of them! Her throat tightened. Her armpits ran cold sweat. Her eyes sparkled. And she never for a single moment questioned her own sanity.

*　　　*　　　*

Twenty-four hours later, John Sheffield was dead. Carried off by a sudden, irreversible congestion of the lungs. And Mary took to her bed suffering from an unaccountable attack of fever which left her pale and shaken to such a degree that Elizabeth sent along one of her own surgeons to bleed the ailing maid. The treatment laid her low for another week, causing her to miss the moment when Robert was given the news. With a shrug of his broad shoulders he spread his hands out in front of him in a gesture of amused resignation.

'None of my doing, I assure you. By God, in turning up his toes the man has placed a veritable yolk about my neck. And one which will no doubt rub me raw on occasion.'

'You could always refuse her,' Kit grinned at him. 'Before it becomes a sore point!'

'True! But first I feel that I should chastise her a little for being so careless with her correspondence.' He laughed indulgently. 'The silly goose could have landed herself in a lot of trouble.' But wasn't it nice to find a woman so besotted, so full of romantic notions, that she had bothered to keep that first note he had written to her? And then to lose it in the middle of a daydream, enabling it to fall into the hands of her irate husband! How Robert loved the absurd femininity of some women. If Elizabeth Tudor had been like Douglass in that respect he would have had her eating out of his hand years ago. Instead, the Queen was so pigheaded when it came to understanding the needs of a lover . . . There was no giggling capitulation there. Only the strength of a general repulsing an enemy! But would Douglass be quite as tempting without the added spice of a husband to deceive? There was only one way to find out. With a wink, he left Kit Hatton chuckling at the turn of events and went to make arrangements for the lady to return to Court as soon as the period of mourning was over.

And Mary Fytton could do nothing but sweat and fume from the stinking confines of her sickbed. Lord Robert had a free hand and plenty of time to provide evidence that the man had died of natural causes. And woe betide anyone who whispered otherwise. There was no one to tittle-tattle to the Queen, and by the time Mary was on her feet again the whole matter was closed.

CHAPTER SIX

'Enough is enough!' Kit Hatton flung the cards down on the table despairingly. 'As usual, Much gets More!' It was the fourth game of 'Tray-trip' in a row he had lost to Robert Dudley in the space of less than half an hour.

'Still waiting for your ship to come in then?'

There was no malice in Robert's teasing. Both he and the Queen had made quite a killing from their investment in John Hawkins's previous voyage and he knew full well that Kit had put every penny he could scrape together into the latest expedition, the largest so far. Six ships had set sail, carrying four hundred men under Hawkins's leadership, complemented by a clutch of eager officers.

'Aye. Is it asking too much, do you think? A profit for a change? Instead of a loss?' It seemed to Kit that he couldn't remember a time when he was not in debt to someone or other. Even back in the early days he had paid for pretty gifts with promises. Ribbons, frills and furbelows. Paltry sums by today's standards, but that was where the rot had started. And once one got used to living in that manner, unfettered by large amounts of money, it quickly became a way of life. But Mister Hatton had his dreams, all of them subconsciously born in the sneering denigration of Mary Fytton. One day he would be rich, and have such standing in the community that she could not help but look up to him. He would be titled, and would build her a palace; a glittering glass case in which he could show her off to perfection. But for the moment these were still ethereal multicoloured fantasies, flitting briefly through his waking hours, and causing him to start from sleep, sweating furiously in the face of failure. It was hard for him to visualize a time when he would be master of a house as grand as the one in which they were now sitting, even if he worked on the sycophantic relationship with Elizabeth till Doomsday. She kept a tight rein on such gratuities.

Robert smiled with the confidence of a man knowing himself in an enviable position.

'I take it you think the upheaval was worth it?'

'Only a fool would think not.' Kit looked around at the sumptuously appointed room in which they sat. Tapestries hung the walls and brilliantly coloured Turkish carpets kept the draughts from the windows in inclement weather. And no stinking rushes rotted on the floor of Lord Robert's withdrawing-room. Instead the beeswaxed wood was covered by a magnificent oriental carpet. Even the Queen did not extend her budget to include this luxury. Nor did she cover her tables with the finest velvet drapes, richly embroidered with gold and silver thread! The chairs on which they were sitting were upholstered in cloth of silver, some shot with green, and some with gold. Even the leather-bound books were thickly ornamented with gilt. The whole of Leicester House was opulence on a grand scale. Opulent, but not isolated. The large, elegant building, built round an inner courtyard and with lawned gardens running smoothly down to a mooring on the great

River Thames, was but a step away from the Stews and playhouses on the periphery of that heaving pool of humanity, London Town. Obtaining the lease from the Paget family had been easy enough, though removing the Spanish Ambassador from such a comfortable dwelling had been more difficult. But as ever, Robert got his way. By order of the Council! And so, in the heat of the summer of 1569 he had finally taken possession of his new establishment on the Strand. Bigger and better by far than Durham House. Fit for an earl. Or a king consort!

A slight movement of Robert's hand was enough to conjure Tamworth up out of thin air, wine in hand, to replenish the cup so recently drained.

'Leave it with us and make sure that we are not disturbed.'

Tamworth bowed respectfully at these orders, his expression blank and unquestioning as ever. He had served his master for many years and his loyalty was without parallel. They would not be disturbed. Nor overheard.

Immediately they were alone Robert stepped across to a cabinet, exquisitely carved from pale, scented wood, and opening it, proceeded to unlock a hidden drawer with a key taken from his pouch. The tiny silver casket which he placed on the table in front of Kit was inlaid with translucent lozenges of glowing amber and decorated with seed pearls set in orange gold. Pure craftsmanship!

'For her?' Kit scarcely needed to ask.

Robert nodded. 'Not just an empty box, either.' Carefully he undid the clasp and lifted the lid to reveal the contents: a crystal vial containing the finest powder imaginable, sparkling like frost inside the tear-drop of glass. He smiled 'Some weeks ago I rode with Meg Clifford down to Mortlake.'

'Doctor Dee?' Kit felt the hairs prickle on his scalp. He feared the superstitions of the ancient wisdoms. They sat badly with his own beliefs. The devil's disciple. That was Doctor Dee. The hand which had been about to reach out for the irresistible beauty of the jewelled box jerked back of its own accord. 'What does it contain?' He leaned back in his chair, as if to distance himself from any spells or charms emanating from the suddenly evil object.

'Don't worry. Nothing to harm you. Or anyone else!' Robert gave him the benefit of a casual, disarming smile. 'The horn of that powerful, magic beast, the unicorn. Guaranteed to nullify the effects of even the most fatal of poisons.'

'Ah . . .' Kit understood immediately. Mary, Queen of Scots, lived in constant fear of sudden death at the hands of her gaolers, and was intelligent enough to realize that poison would make an ideal end to her if her cousin Elizabeth so chose. If she had been allowed to meet the Queen of England face to face things would have been different. Then she could have persuaded her that she had nothing to fear, and that Mary only wanted to rule her own lands in the north. But it had not happened. So it was time to think of other things. Of other ways out of her predicament. Of other kingdoms to rule. In the south!

'De Spes has already made himself known to her.' The new Spanish Ambassador had lost no time in proposing an alliance between his master and the prisoner. A Catholic alliance. 'And we must be ready with our own proposals before the scheming gets out of hand. And of course, secrecy is essential!' Robert wanted no word of his involvement in any such plot reaching the ears of Elizabeth. 'I can count on you? Beg leave to visit your lands in Northampton . . . and forget to halt until you reach Sheffield Castle.'

The two men faced each other across the gleaming facets of the heathen reliquary, one, black-haired, black-eyed, and with a strong, compelling gaze; the other, sporting soft brown hair and sapphire eyes which flinched with indecision. Kit Hatton looked away.

'*I* cannot go. Elizabeth knows my every move. And Norfolk is persuaded. He is determined to marry Mary, given half a chance. God knows, I would if I could!' Robert managed to look like a child who sees his sugar-plum stolen from under his nose.

An alternative Catholic marriage! Far better

an Englishman than a foreigner! And the chance to meet Queen Mary . . . and gain a firmer foothold in that camp . . . just in case! Kit began to see the advantages to be gained by such a move.

Robert could read acceptance in his face. 'The abdication must be cancelled, of course. And Mary's marriage to Boswell ended. He has fled to Denmark, in any case, and is unlikely to return.'

Unlikely to live. The same thought was in both men's minds.

'And assuming that she is willing to ratify the Treaty of Edinburgh, she will be pronounced heiress presumptive to the throne of England. What do you say?'

Kit nodded slowly. If all parties were in agreement . . . would Elizabeth be persuaded that Mary's nomination was only right and proper? It would put an end to the interminable speculation; to the wrangles in the Council. But why was Robert Dudley so adamant that the plan should succeed? Where was his reward? What did a Puritan hope to gain from such a manoeuvre?

Robert anticipated the question. 'With the succession at last settled, England may look more favourably on the marriage of our own Queen . . . to a mere earl! Mary already has a son, so Doctor Huiks's opinion that Elizabeth will never bear children in any event will no longer matter.' But whilst Elizabeth lived, her husband would rule. King Consort in name. But King in truth. And if Norfolk put so much as one little toe out of line! Elizabeth had committed no one to the block so far in her reign, but should it be at all necessary, then Thomas Howard's neck would be an admirable place to start.

The headsman's axe had no place in Kit's thoughts. Unlike Robert, he had no personal knowledge of this gruesome and extremely bloody form of dying. Francis Hatton had died of natural causes. But Robert's handsome brother Guildford had strolled, still proud and arrogant, to feel the cold blade strike and strike again in the heat of a summer day. And Robert had waited, in company with the remaining sons of the great John Dudley, for the call which never came. By a miracle he had been spared, and now, years later, and closer to the Queen than any man alive, he felt himself immune from the consquences of treason. So far as Kit was concerned, such goings-on belonged to the bad old days; to another time; another reign; another queen. The only thought in his mind was of how far he had come in so short a space of time. From a gauche young student, more interested in acting than in Law, to a favourite of Elizabeth Tudor. And now more than that: he was about to become part of the intrigue which surrounded the monarchy. Confidant of the Earl of Leicester, Saviour of Mary, Queen of

Scots! If the plan worked and he found that he had indeed been instrumental in bringing about the marriage of the Scottish queen and the foremost Duke of England, and so opening the way for Robert to marry Elizabeth at last . . . There would be nothing he could not have as a reward. Nothing! A title would be his for the asking. The Palace of Holdenby, to date, nothing more than a dream, would most definitely be built. And Mary . . . Mary would run willingly into his waiting arms!

'Hrmmph!' Robert cleared his throat. 'You'll do it then?'

Kit raised his head slowly, the blue of his eyes holding a steely glint which hit Robert forcefully. For the first time he recognized true ambition in this athletic young courtier. The indecision had gone and the iron grip of his hand showed a determination to succeed.

'Willingly!'

'Then with the jewelled casket, take this.'

Robert took a folded letter from inside his doublet and without looking too closely Kit knew that the seal which fastened it was that of Thomas Howard, Duke of Norfolk. The plans were obviously well advanced. All they had been short of was a courier. But his days of dithering on the fringe of politics were over. There was no turning back now. Christopher Hatton had made up his mind!

* * *

'Am I really growing old, do you think?' Elizabeth held the silver mirror up before her face, illuminated by the early morning light of a perfect summer day. She knew her complexion to be flawless but perhaps . . .? Were those lines of worry round her eyes?

'You know full well that women half your age envy you your beauty.' Mary laughed at the absurdity of her mistress. In so many ways she was as strong as any man, and yet, deep down she suffered from a childish insecurity. 'Your skin is softer than the smallest child's, and there is not one single grey hair in your head. You are not old.' Mary's voice softened to a whisper as she continued to brush the Queen's waist-length hair. 'You are in the prime of your life and more beautiful than at any time before.'

With the speed of a viper striking its prey, the Queen's slim, tapered fingers fastened on Mary's wrist, well-tended nails digging into soft flesh like vicious, poisonous fangs.

'Then why am I being avoided? Why, suddenly will no one look me in the eye? If I haven't become warty overnight, what is it?' The feminine fragility was a lie, as Mary well knew. Having indulged in a variety of outdoor sports, often equalling her courtiers, Elizabeth's willowy figure hid all the strength of an oak.

With a squeal of pain Mary submitted to the

intense pressure and sank to her knees, her face contorted in agony.

'Why?'

Another cruel twist left the maid gasping as tears started in her eyes.

'Norfolk!' Mary blurted out the word as her expression pleaded for release.

The Queen relaxed her hold. 'Norfolk? What about Norfolk?'

'They . . . He plans to marry your cousin of Scotland.'

Elizabeth caught the initial hesitation. 'They?' She looked sharply at the young woman sitting in a crumpled heap at her feet. 'Who are they?'

'I don't know. I'm not sure . . .' Mary's voice faltered as she saw the Queen's eyes narrow.

'Once more, Mary. Who are they?'

'The Council . . . Cecil . . . Lord Robert, perhaps. I don't know for certain. Truly I don't.'

She was telling the truth. Meg Clifford had told her the tale, having been asked to procure a special vial of Horn of Unicorn from Doctor Dee which could be used as an antidote to poison: to assure the Scottish queen of friendship at Elizabeth's Court. A vial which had been delivered to Robert! Meg had her own way of finding out snippets of information in the shape of Tamworth, the Earl of Leicester's body-servant, and she was rarely wrong. But the last thing Mary Fytton wanted to do was implicate Meg in what could become a dangerous escapade. But by all accounts, Tamworth had been sent on an errand to collect a letter from Thomas Howard himself which he had delivered to his master.

Elizabeth stared at her maid suspiciously. Did she know more? Then the frown cleared. No matter! Now that she had some idea of the things afoot in the Council Chamber it would be easy enough to keep a weather-eye on them. It was as well to be forewarned of a storm brewing!

Silently Mary examined the bruises beginning to shadow her wrist. Blood seeped slowly from the broken skin, vivid scarlet against its paleness. A sudden awareness of the damage she had inflicted broke through Elizabeth's thoughts as she encountered the soulful gaze of the kneeling woman. A bewildered puppy. Hurt, yet still anxious to please.

'Mary. Oh, Mary! Forgive me.'

Tentatively the maid offered the injured arm to her mistress, the pain showing in her eyes indicating that she too asked forgiveness. Physical pain meant nothing. All she asked was to serve.

Elizabeth licked away the blood, tasting the salt. Blood and tears mingled as she kissed the discoloured skin. Kissed it better, as though Mary was only a child, before drawing her close and rocking the shaking girl tenderly in her arms. How difficult it was sometimes to mete out harsh treatment. And yet it was necessary. Even with Mary. As a queen she dared not let anyone gain the upper hand or she knew that her powers would soon be undermined, and there was no shortage of pretenders to the throne. And this whimpering woman could be counted in their number, she reminded herself. Not that Mary would ever try a trick like that. She had too much to be grateful to Elizabeth for. As for these secret dealings between Thomas Howard and Mary Stewart . . . There was no sense in rushing in . . . Give them enough rope and they would hang themselves.

And so the Queen waited in expectation of being told, eventually, of the plans, but the summer drew on and not a single word was said on the subject in her presence. Perhaps it really was some kind of plot? The Court moved to Richmond during August and on a sultry afternoon which threatened thunder Elizabeth almost let the matter slip her tongue.

'Will it rain, do you think? Or are we to endure another airless night?' A thin film of sweat glistened on Elizabeth's forehead, despite the fan with which she attempted to cool her face. The dress of every woman present was being unavoidably spoilt by damp, dark stains beneath the arms, and in some cases the whole of the bodice ran wet and reeking.

'Oh, I do hope so.' Anne Grey, being plumper than most, was all but fainting with a combination of the heat and the tightness of her garments. 'Though I admit that a heavy downpour would bring havoc to the gardens. And prevent our exercise.' Knowing how the Queen liked to be out and about the girl tried her best to seem dismayed by this prospect though everyone knew that she would much rather be tucked up somewhere cosy with a plate of honeycakes or fruit tarts.

'Then shall we collect flowers to take inside? We can bring the garden in to keep us company.' Lady Clinton glanced up at the sky. The sun still shone but menacing black clouds were rapidly gathering over the horizon and it would be as well if they started to make their way back to the palace before too long.

The Queen nodded her approval and several of her maids disappeared into the distance, chattering nineteen to the dozen as they argued over where to begin. Elizabeth smiled. If only that was all *she* had to worry about! At that moment, as though conjured up by her thoughts, Thomas Howard strolled into view, obviously unaware of the Queen or her ladies. His mind was elsewhere as Elizabeth studied him. Not handsome. And too solemn. Life seemed so serious from the Duke of Norfolk's position. The Queen sighed. Thank God all her courtiers were not made like him.

That would produce a very dull and boring world.

'My dear Thomas!' Her joyous welcome indicated a pleasure which was practised rather than heartfelt.

Thomas was startled out of his introspective composure by the sound. His face appeared to pale in the heat as his grey-green eyes flicked uneasily, looking for a way of escape. There was none. Better make the best of a bad job then. Forcing his mouth into the semblance of a smile he ambled forward jerkily to bow low over the Queen's outstretched hand.

'Your Majesty. More lovely than ever in this sylvan setting. More elegant than the tallest tree. Prettier than . . .'

The Queen cut his flattery short with a dismissive wave of her fingers. 'Too hot, Thomas. Far too hot for idle chit-chat. Come. Walk with me in the shade a while and entertain me with the wit and rhetoric I have come to expect from my men.'

Thomas's disquiet grew. She had to be jesting with him. Wit? That was hardly his forté. Had Elizabeth heard anything of the communication which had been going on between him and her prisoner in the north of England?

Elizabeth was indeed making fun of the man. Three years younger than her own thirty-six, he seemed already more staid and pedantic than many a one nearing their dotage. This was perhaps understandable if his disastrous personal life was considered. He had, after all, buried three wives! But was he as far advanced in his quest for a fourth as the Queen believed?

'Forgive me. Your Majesty . . . I am at a loss . . .' The poor man wiped rapidly at the sudden moisture springing from every pore. The embroidered linen was a sodden mess in no time.

But Elizabeth was determined to give him every opportunity to vindicate himself and show that his motives were not subversive in any way.

'Then tell me, are you now over the worst of your grief? How long is it since Elizabeth died?'

'Almost two years, Your Majesty. But fortunately, time is a great healer.'

'Ah! Then are you plagued by offers, as I am? Who is it wishes to become the next Duchess of Norfolk? You know that I shall be pleased to consent to any suitable match.'

Was there a slight emphasis on the word 'suitable'? Dear Lord, she must know. This Court was the very devil for trying to keep anything secret. Or was his guilt making him read more into her words than was meant? What should he do? Make a clean breast of it? But that temper of hers! If she hadn't guessed . . . ? Best leave well alone. Just in case. Thunder rumbled in the distance. Storm clouds were gathering, and Thomas shivered in the heat.

'Look, Your Majesty. Aren't they beautiful?'

The silence, which had been getting too long for comfort, was broken by the melodious tones of Lady Clinton and the happy chatter of the other ladies. A basket of flowers was held up for Elizabeth to inspect. Marguerites, marigolds and forget-me-nots, lavender and poppy. A colourful display which distracted the Queen from the Duke and his mumbled stammerings for long enough to give him an excuse. With a perfunctory bow and a 'by your leave' he was gone, slinking away beneath the hedges as though terrified at being recalled. The Queen let him go.

Thomas was in such a state of nerves after the encounter that he confided his fears to Robert at the first opportunity and, as the Court progressed, the Earl of Leicester used all his subtlety and charm to investigate Elizabeth's true feelings on the matter of the marriage. The signs were not unfavourable and he advised Thomas to speak up. And the sooner the better for all concerned! The Duke of Norfolk, however, was succeeding in convincing himself that the Catholic strength in the north of England was sufficient to overcome all obstacles in his path. If only he could rescue Queen Mary from her unfortified prison at Winfield . . . He was making plans which even Robert had no idea about.

But Robert Dudley was no one's fool. No one, not even Cecil, had more spies than he did. As the Court moved on from Guildford to Hampshire, keeping ahead of the filth and unappetizing stench left behind by such a large and unmanageable household, he decided that the time had come for him to withdraw from what looked for all the world like a plot to overthrow Elizabeth. Kit Hatton sighed with relief. He was new to the intrigue and double-dealing and, now that the first flush of excitement at being involved had worn off he was beginning to have nightmares, seeing himself chased round and round Tower Green by the executioner. Screaming as the axe sliced through his flesh. Perhaps he wasn't destined to be a politician! Perhaps he should settle for a quiet life. With Nan. If only he had the courage he would tell the Queen himself and put an end to nervous speculation . . . No use! He was even more of a coward than Thomas, bearing in mind how much the Duke had to gain from speaking up and confessing!

Eventually it was Robert who took matters into his own hands and retired to his bed with a mysterious illness, showing every symptom of imminent death. But it was not a priest he called for. It was a Queen. Exactly what he revealed to her no-one knew, but when Thomas Howard left the Court to make final plans in London, Elizabeth was ready for him.

The premature uprising in the north was

squashed and an unhappy Norfolk found ample time to reflect on his mistakes as he languished in the Tower. Far more time than the seven hundred peasants who paid with their lives. But less than Mary, Queen of Scots would have in the fortress of Tutbury. There would be no escape. Ever.

This whole episode had an unsettling effect on the Court. After such a period of tension laced with subterfuge and treason, during which the Queen had deftly kept one step ahead of the game and summoned up the stamina to work long hours with little sleep, she at last succumbed to bouts of debilitating migraine. Mary Fytton was with her constantly, applying soothing compresses in the quiet privacy of a darkened room. It was the opportunity the maid had been waiting for. Always insecure in her position, she now felt positively threatened. Elin von Snakenburg played the lute so sweetly that Elizabeth had taken to having the girl on a cushion at her feet, popping sugar-plums and other sweetmeats into the child's mouth as rewards. And fondling the silken skeins of platinum hair. Mary would have willingly throttled the prissy miss if she could have done it without detection. Jealousy gnawed constantly at her guts. But how could she be rid of the Queen's little snowdrop? How could it be crushed? Ruined? Then an idea dawned. Marriage! That was surely the answer! And Mary knew the very man!

'I am worried, Your Majesty, about . . .' Mary hesitated. 'About Lord Northampton . . .'

'Worried? How?' Elizabeth rested comfortably against the mound of pillows in a deeply shadowed room.

'He . . . he seems so lonely. So alone. Missing a wife, and the lack making him old before his time, poor man.'

'He has not mentioned marriage . . .' But then would he? William, like his sister Katherine before him, would not burden his Queen with problems unnecessarily. Especially during a year of plots and intrigue. And how understandable that Mary should be concerned for William Parr's welfare. She could be so thoughtful.

'And who would you suggest to make dear William happy again?'

'You haven't noticed?' Mary deliberately sounded surprised. 'I thought the whole Court had realized how smitted he is with little Elin. She seems to be the only one who can make him smile.'

'Elin? Are you sure?' The Queen was taken aback. And yet . . . if anything were to happen to Elizabeth . . . Yes. The girl needed a protector; someone to provide her with an income. And where would she find a gentler, kinder husband? A man who would be more father than lover? Probably incapable of being a lover! The Queen patted Mary's hand indulgently. 'You're right, of course. William will be far happier with a wife, and Elin more secure with a protector. An excellent solution to both their problems. And a wedding will lift us all from the doldrums!'

For Robert it was a great relief to put the unfortunate Norfolk episode behind him, and during the celebrations he was able to relax for the first time in many a day. Both he and Kit were on their best behaviour, though by the end of the evening the consumption of a large quantity of wine was beginning to have its effect.

'Ah, marriage!' Robert leaned against Kit, his arm about his friend's shoulders. 'Does Northampton know what he is about, do you think?'

They watched the stiff old gentleman in his pathetic efforts to execute a caper, determined to please his child-bride. Or die in the attempt! Elin was spring to his winter. Dressed in an exquisite gown of silver, embroidered with the palest of leaf-green silks and oversewn with pearls, she had the translucent beauty of a fairy-queen. Delicate. Ethereal. By contrast, her husband looked worn-out beyond his years, stooped and none too steady on his feet. His face was flushed scarlet and his eyes bright as he devoured the sight of her, his imagination of the delights ahead almost bringing him to apoplexy before the whole Court.

'Will he live to enjoy it to the full?' Kit hiccupped as he spoke. 'Pardon me! And more to the point, shall we? Where is our wedded bliss, dear fellow?'

The two men gazed forlornly across the room at the royal dais. Elizabeth sat enthroned, glittering from head to foot with a fortune in jewels, her dress rigid with the magnificence of solid gold worked into the cloth. Emeralds and pearls adorned her hair, tortured into the high fashion now favoured by the women, thrown into relief by the ornate ruff which rose twelve inches high, surrounding her head with a halo of open embroidery and lace. And behind her, a foil to her fair colouring, stood Mary Fytton. Ravenhaired and vibrant, dressed in glowing scarlet velvet, her only ornament, a single ruby pendant, sparkling between her breasts with every movement.

The wine the men had drunk blurred their minds to any faults they might have found yesterday in those two women. Through an alcoholic haze they were perfection. The Queen watched the bride and groom benevolently. And Mary! She seemed to have lost her normal vindictiveness completely and was smiling like the cat who had got the cream. Delicious. Delectable. Kit felt the inevitable stirring in his loins. He groaned audibly.

'As bad as that? Despite Nan?' Robert staggered slightly and would have fallen but for the fact that he still had his arm around Kit.

'You should know. Whilst you have been eyeing the Queen, Douglass has watched your every move.'

Robert's eyes flickered towards his mistress momentarily.

'Aye. She has things on her mind. Marriage. As we were saying. But I told her when this affair started. Out of the question! And she agreed. Then! Now it seems, she has changed her mind. Marriage! With the Queen still tantalizingly within my reach? Or is she? Will she ever, do you think?'

'Don't ask me. If she is anything like her maid, then the answer is no. Neither of them will ever lie panting with desire in a marriage bed.' He grinned drunkenly. 'So it's Douglass for you. And Nan for me. And we might as well make it tonight. In secret.' His hiccups were getting the better of him. 'What would your lady say to that?'

'I've no doubt that she would be highly delighted, but Kit, my friend, where are we to get a sober cleric tonight? At such short notice? And how shall I feel about the matter in the morning?'

'Better, I trust. And you will be free of complaints from her ladyship. Robert Wilmot now has a place in Canon Row, being given more to the Cloth than to Law these days and . . .'

'Wilmot will never consent to conduct a secret marriage for fear of the Queen,' Robert interrupted.

'If you will let me finish! Our friend is away at present and his rooms are free, and we have never been short of actors in our company . . .'

'A pretence?' The light was beginning to dawn. 'And let Douglass think that . . . Ha! That would put an end to her nagging. Make her every bit as compliant as she was in the woods at Belvoir. But we should have to impress on her the need to keep the event from reaching the ears of the Queen or the joke may backfire . . .'

'Stop worrying. Imagine the night you will spend! Imagine the reward you will reap in her grateful arms! Nothing will be denied you . . . You go whisper in the lady's ear, and I shall find a man who fancies himself temporarily in Holy Orders.'

Several hours later some sort of commotion in the street outside her window disturbed Nan Hobson from her slumbers. What was it? What was all the shouting about? Kit? It sounded like his voice. Pulling a woollen shawl about the shoulders of her nightgown she stumbled, still half asleep, to open the shutters.

'Come down, woman. Come now and I shall make an honest woman of you. Come on, come on! I only make the offer once!'

'You're drunk, Mister Hatton, or you

wouldn't make a fool of me in this way. Honest woman indeed! Lower your voice before you have the constables on your tail. There now!' she muttered crossly. 'You have woken the child with your nonsense. Are you coming up or shall you sleep off your madness elsewhere?'

Kit pursed his lips and nodded to himself. That was his Nan. Steady as a rock. Down to earth. Not one to be swept off her feet. Never again. Not since Midsummer Meadow. The only impetuous thing she had ever done in her life.

'Pah! Don't come crying to me in the morning then. And don't say that I never gave you the chance.' With a loud hiccup which echoed down the otherwise silent street, he turned away. If she wouldn't then she wouldn't and that was the end of it.

With an amused smile Nan watched him go. He'd have a headache and a half by morning and remember nothing of his midnight revels, like as not. Did little boys ever really grow up, she wondered? But if Mistress Hobson was too sensible to be taken in by a ridiculous reveller well into his cups, Douglass Howard was only too eager to be deceived by the farcical arrangements. She wanted to believe it, and that was the difference. The Queen had not given the necessary permission, so the contract would have to remain secret. This she fully understood. But at least she was Robert's wife at last. No longer just a frivolous mistress. A wife! Douglass made up her mind there and then to live up to her new title by becoming more refined and matronly as befitted her station. Robert would be proud of her. She would show him that she was more than simply a pretty face and his household would be run more efficiently than he ever thought possible.

So it came about that the Earl of Leicester remained a bachelor but found himself living with a veritable wife, which was hardly the outcome he had expected. And Kit thanked his lucky stars that Nan had more sense in her little finger than he had in his head, on occasion, all of which did not prevent him from dreaming his dreams and continuing to insist that they came true. And the Palace of Holdenby came high on his list.

On a visit to his native county, Christopher Hatton encountered the man who declared that he could make that very dream come true. John Thorpe, architect and surveyor, had been engaged by Sir Humphrey Stafford, a neighbour of the Hattons, to build a majestic house at Kirby, a mere eight miles distant. A building which was being talked of county-wide. This, and Mister Thorpe's natural eloquence persuaded Kit that the time was ripe to set in motion his own grand designs. Despite the fact that Hawkins had not yet brought home the bounty.

The palace would, he thought, be raised a

few steps above the general level, and built around two great courts, one with a colonnade. There was to be a Great Hall and a long gallery, a chapel and high stone archways leading to the walled gardens and the spinneys beyond. A building of light and sunshine, full of windows. And the greatest talking point of all, the inclusion of magnificent turrets at the corners of the first court. Looking at the site, Kit imagined how it would stand, proud and solid, gazing out over his lands. Northamptonshire. The fairest county in all England. And here Mary would dwell, with every luxury at her fingertips. Mistress of the most imposing property in the land, excepting only Hampton Court. And himself? A man of substance at last!

How could he have possibly known that the Spanish had routed Hawkins's fleet? Or that Drake had fled the scene to make his excuses to Her Majesty, leaving the leader to limp behind, a tattered remnant of its former glory. When the brave but beaten flagship at last reached English shores there were only ten men left alive on board. If men they could be called. Animals, more like, after the horror and hardship they had endured! And all hopes of wealth for Kit Hatton had sunk without trace. He would never, as long as he lived, manage to get out of the enormous debt his fanciful aspirations had landed him in.

*   *   *

Warm breezes riffled thick summer foliage against a cloudless sky as the lark soared effortlessly on rising columns of air. His song, clear and joyous, was lost in the hubbub and general clamour of the jostling throng clustered below him in the vicinity of Tower Hill. A motley jumble. A sea of heads rippling in constant motion. Nearer at hand from ground level, Kit eyed his fellow loiterers curiously. They came from all walks of life.

A merchant, arm in arm with his wife, showed his prosperity as much in his portly belly and the quivering bulk of his mate as he did in the cut and quality of his clothes. They strutted by, a pair of pouter pigeons, preening themselves publicly in an effort to be envied. The consumptive beggar boy, death already etching purple shadows under his enormous melancholic eyes was treated to a contemptuous sniff, gratis. Nothing more was forthcoming from Mistress Merchant. What she had she clung to with pitiless devotion. Kit squeezed a coin into the ignored, upturned palm. God grant the child time enough to spend it on some small enjoyment. Sweethearts, hand in hand, ran by on tiptoe, laughing into each other's eyes as they seemed to walk on air, he, in leather jerkin and hose, and she, in autumn-coloured fustian. Ordinary folk. Young and happy on a summer day.

The scaffold drew Kit's gaze like a magnet. Raw wood. Clean. Unsullied. A monument to failure. He shivered in the sun, feeling sick to his stomach for the ordeal about to be faced by Thomas Howard, Duke of Norfolk.

'For your good lady, sir. A ribbon for her hair. A pin. A lover's knot.' The tinker's hopeful smile revealed a mouthful of crooked, blackened stumps. He winked suggestively. 'A garter for her knee?'

Kit turned away. Was this really no more than a carnival? A parade to air one's Sunday best? Or beg a crust? Or sell a bauble? The rich nap of a velvet suit flashed momentarily through a brief gap in the crowd. The young Earl of Oxford, unless he was very much mistaken, now a member of Gray's Inn. And where Edward de Vere was, there would be others of that ilk. Forcing a way into and beyond the crush of London's flotsam, he found that he was not mistaken. Nicholas Hilliard, the young man whose miniatures were becoming all the rage, and George Gascoigne, the latest up-and-coming playwright, stood alongside Henry Noel and John Popham.

The latter had no complaints about the unusual occurrence. In fact, he had much to be grateful for, Robert Dudley giving him this chance to make his name in the Law Courts. And make a profit at the same time! But for most, the thought of Thomas, whom they had known all their adult lives, losing his head, had a numbing effect. And that feeling was not confined to this group of men. The signature on the warrant had cost Elizabeth dear. After dithering for days her councillors had finally persuaded her that it was the only course open to her. She couldn't let both Thomas and Mary Stewart live after the treason they had plotted together. One of them would have to pay!

Henry nodded a greeting as Kit joined the group. 'So you decided to come after all?'

'Aye. There was little point in staying away. The Queen wanted only her women around her. She wouldn't even let Robert stay, or even say a few words of comfort. I decided that it would be worse trying to live with my imagination than witnessing the deed.'

'The Queen is still suffering then?' George Gascoigne raised an eyebrow. 'She's not made like her father. He'd sign away five before breakfast and then ride out with the hunt.'

'You forget. One he rid himself of was Elizabeth's own mother. She's lived in the shadow of the axe all her life and is known to have nightmares about meeting the same fate herself. Surely one of the reasons she hasn't married? Whilst she is in sole control she has nothing to lose from our masked friend here.' Nicholas had seen the man arrive, muscular arms running sweat with nervous agitation. He'd practised for long hours on logs, each cut to the thickness of a man's neck. But how would he fare with the real thing? If he bungled it the Duke was sure to scream and the executioner was terrified of losing his nerve, failing to despatch the prisoner. It had been known. In the old days.

The crowd froze, to a man, necks craned and eyes strained, all in the same direction, as though they played a game in which the first to move would be disqualified. In the sudden silence the purity of the lark's solo anthem was enriched by a blackbird's harmonious descant from the lofty choir of a nearby oak. A brief illusion of peace. Shattered by the throb of a drum, its steady beat heralding the main event of the day. The watchers held their breath expectantly, gagged by morbid fascination. Thomas Howard stepped forward.

Their eyes met. Kit felt the rest of the world recede beyond his vision as the Duke's helpless incredulity washed over him. The man still couldn't, even in his final moment, believe that it was the end. Others had been involved. Kit had carried that first vital message giving the Scottish queen a reason to hope. To plot. And the great mind behind the whole thing? Where was Robert today? Not standing on the freshly split planks from which the new gallows had been hurriedly fashioned. Not kneeling to examine at close quarters the unseasoned wood. To smell the sharp sap odour baking under a hot June sun. To know that the axe was being raised.

Kit lowered his gaze to the lush grasses, now trampled and bruised beneath his feet. The first blow had failed to sever the head from the body. The second too. An elastic complex of flesh, sinew and bone does not crack apart like a dry log. Sweat blinded the headsman as he lifted his weapon a third time. A cheer forced Kit to conquer cowardice and he watched with horror as a disembodied head was held triumphantly aloft, leaving great gobbits of blood congealing around the still twitching body.

'Oh my God, because You are so good, I am very sorry that I have sinned against Thee and with the help of Thy Grace I will not sin again.' The words came automatically to Kit's lips. John Popham cleared his throat as Kit continued, seemingly oblivious to his surroundings.

'Hail Mary, Mother of God. Hail Mary full of Grace. The Lord is with thee . . .'

'Kit? Are you all right?' Henry Noel took his arm and began leading his friend away from the carnage. The others followed, each lost in his own thoughts. Some would have more to fear than others if Elizabeth took a liking to such blood sports but who knew where it would all end? The sooner the better life returned to normal, or at least that today's events were pushed into the background. Glossed over.

'I have a new play written . . .' George

Gascoigne was the first to break the silence, 'which is perhaps just the thing to take Her Majesty's mind from treason. What is Robert's company up to at the moment? Are they available to learn the lines? Are they in town? Kit?'

With an effort Kit roused himself from his shocked state, coming to the conclusion that compared to some, he must be singularly lacking in spirit. Or ambition. Living alongside ruthless men like Norfolk, and Robert, he had become caught up in a way of life which did not come naturally to him, bringing all sorts of worries and anxieties which he had never looked for, and which he could very well do without. Jousting, tilting and sword-play. Acting and dancing. These were the things at which he excelled. But some women expected more than that from their menfolk! For some women, only the best would do! And yet those were the very things which Elizabeth admired him for, and it was possible that if he concentrated on the activities he did best, he would attain his goal. Some day.

'Aye. They are down at the Cross Keys, performing to enthusiastic crowds daily, though I doubt Robert will be there at this time of day. I have business with him anyway so I shall put your idea to him and meet you there later. Agreed?'

Kit knew that Robert was not with the Queen so he made his way to Leicester House, doggedly refusing to dwell on the sights and sounds to which he had been witness, but conscious of them lurking in the back of his mind, waiting to surprise him. The gardens of Robert's house were deserted, shimmering in the heat and heavy with the scents of summer. The building too, seemed strangely silent; asleep in the afternoon heat. It would appear that the master of the house was not at home.

Douglass Sheffield, sitting alone, watching swans glide by on the River Thames, welcomed him with a wan smile and a raised eyebrow. The perfect hostess, she immediately sent for refreshment.

'This is a pleasant, but unexpected diversion.' She was not entirely insensible to Christopher Hatton's physical attractions. A pity he was untitled though. Yet if he had been, Robert would have been faced with a very formidable rival for the Queen's affections and the two most handsome men at Elizabeth's Court could never have been the friends they were. 'But I take it that I am not the reason for your journey.'

Kit kissed her hand graciously. 'I would disagree with you but for the fact that I would not have Robert thinking that I deliberately creep into his house whilst he is not at home. He is not at home?'

'No,' Douglass shook her head. 'I . . . I don't know where he is.'

Her look was guarded; the expression in her

eyes, uneasy. And Kit had noticed that the nails of the hand he had raised to his mouth suffered from excessive biting. They looked red and painful enough to be infected. Why? What was Robert up to now?

'If he isn't with you, he must be with the Queen.' She saw from Mister Hatton's face that this was not so. 'Or maybe he has duties on Tower Hill?'

'That must be it.' Kit had noticed a certain dampness beginning to moisten her lashes as her mouth stiffened in an effort to prevent her lips from trembling. He studied her as he sipped the wine he had been offered. What had happened to the giggling little poppet his friend had seduced away from John Sheffield? She was modestly dressed, and thinking about it, that was not a word he would have used to describe Douglass a couple of years ago. Modest she had never been. She was no longer following the extremes of fashion; no longer eye-catching or obviously selling her wares to the highest bidder. Her hair was neat, and her gown neater. A woman settled in her home. Reliable. Dull! But she must surely have realized that she had changed? And that Robert hadn't! So who was he with today to take his mind from funerals? Kit had no intention of listening to Douglass's tales of woe if he could help it so, making his excuses, he left her, somewhat abruptly.

If Robert really was with another woman he

could be anywhere in London. It would be like looking for a needle in a haystack, but one thing was certain: sooner or later he would be at Elizabeth's side with soothing words of friendship and comfort. So with that thought in mind Kit made his way back to Court.

There, however, he met with as little success as he had at Leicester House. The hall was empty except for a couple of hounds asleep and twitching in a shaft of sunlight. In the corridors, nothing stirred. Once, he saw a servant girl tripping earnestly back to the kitchens but for all the interest she showed, he might have been invisible. Then she was swallowed up by the gloom; as though she had been nothing more than a figment of his imagination. He had the oddest sensation that he was the only person left on earth. The rest of humanity had been spirited away. Or maybe they had never existed! Perhaps he had dreamed it all. Kit wondered whether he was going mad; whether the blood and gore of the morning had addled his brain.

The Queen's apartments were as deserted as the rest of the place. Frustration made him tense as he wandered from room to room until at last he flopped down in an ingle-nook seat cosily piled with cushions and shielded from the rest of the small, private closet by an embroidered fire-screen and an aromatic arrangement of summer herbs and flowers. Enough of this chasing around on such a day.

He would wait for the world to come to him!

Sleep claimed him. Mary ran towards him across daisy-spangled grass, arms outstretched and eager. The scent of lavender filled the air and a cock crowed in the distance. Dawn! Her velvet gown became transformed into the tattered shift with its ragged hem worn to such effect by his lovely gipsy girl.

'Mary!'

She was in his embrace, responsive and warm. Essentially female. Giving. Loving. And then the axe swung down from the heavens. A silver-honed edge, slicing through the air. If they hadn't parted to let it pass between them . . .

How long he had slept he was never to know. It was the gentle sobbing of a heart-broken woman which interrupted his dreams, a sound so soft that he awakened slowly to find himself gazing in bewilderment through his fragrant shield of rosemary and thyme.

'Don't, Elizabeth. Don't blame yourself. There was nothing else you could do.'

The intimate familiarity with which these words were spoken snapped his eyelids open wide. Mary Fytton! And the Queen! That was the moment he should have made himself known, but something held him back. The tone of her voice? Curiosity? He didn't know. But after that crucial hesitation there was nothing he could do. Except hold his breath and pray that he was not discovered.

'Please. This isn't like you.' Mary sounded as though she was about to burst into tears herself.

'And that's the pity of it. There are so many times when I wish that life could have been different. If I could have been man instead of woman! Or never born at all!' Elizabeth sniffed into the linen square. 'I have a duty to be strong and strong I shall be. But I am human.'

'I know. I know.' Mary put her arm about Elizabeth's waist. 'More human and understanding than any other creature on God's earth. More human than many of your subjects deserve.'

The two women looked deep into each other's eyes, and Elizabeth wondered for the thousandth time whether her suspicions about her own origins had any basis in truth. She remembered vividly the day old Elizabeth Fytton had brought Mary to Court and how, for the first time in her life she had plucked up the courage to ask about her mother. Mistress Fytton had been her mother's maid, right up until that last day. She had also been the mistress of William Brereton, the courtier accused, amongst others, of adultery with Anne Boleyn. If anyone knew the truth, Elizabeth Fytton did. So was it her imagination, or had the old crone really hinted that the Queen of England was not the daughter of Henry? She had appeared to be in a trance; to have the Sight. And she had insisted that Elizabeth Tudor was born to be Queen. The greatest queen the world has ever known. So even if . . . even if Will Brereton had played an important part in the history of his country . . . it had been ordained. By the gods. She was born to be Queen. But never to give birth. She could never, in all conscience, perpetuate the line. And Mary. She too would never breed; never be allowed to produce a child which could possibly have a greater claim to the throne than the woman now upon it. But in any case, Mary Fytton hated to be touched by a man.

'Is the door locked?'

Mary moved across the floor silently to check. Then they were in each other's arms, locked in a passionate embrace; in a kiss so hungry with desire that it seemed it would never end. Their hands caressed. Undressed. Unintelligible endearments were whispered between sighs of ecstasy. And Kit Hatton hid his face in the cushions, choking with incredulity and disgust.

* * *

His friends waited at the Cross Keys in vain. Kit visited instead the sleazy end of town, looking for oblivion; sour ale was downed with sweet. It was all the same to him. The whore he paid was scarcely more than a child, yet when it came to the point, and she stood, skirts raised obligingly, against the wall, he turned away, sickened. So many things had suddenly fallen into place. And what a fool he had been making of himself all this time! Mary must have laughed herself silly at his antics. And no wonder she had warned him that the Queen would be displeased. That was an understatement! Poor Robert . . . Then he thought again. Poor Robert nothing! He had not sat celibate and pining whilst he awaited the Queen's pleasure. From the fear in Douglass's eyes, he had more than enough to keep him well exercised. And what had Mister Hatton to show for all his years at Court? Debts! Debts, and more debts. No mansion. No wife. No title. He felt his stomach rumble in rebellion as he attempted to swallow more ale and before he could so much as move it spewed its contents into the morass of straw and dog shit on the floor. It was time to go home. Pissing into the gutter, he found that a comforting thought. Silver Street. The nearest thing to home he had ever known.

Nan Hobson cleaned him up as best she could before half carrying him to the bed. He'd been drunk many a time, but never like this. Kit wasn't one of the Court rowdies, given to extravagant displays of drinking prowess to prove his manhood. He was, she knew, the most gentle of gentlemen. Something must have upset his applecart today and no mistake.

Perhaps the execution . . .

She couldn't tell what time it was when she woke, disturbed by that sixth sense; knowing that he was no longer beside her in the bed. In the moonlight's subtle glow he almost blended with the shadows of the room.

'Kit?' There was no answer.

'Kit, are you all right?'

It was the second time today someone had asked him that. He didn't move. Of course he was all right. Why shouldn't he be? The day had been nothing out of the ordinary. Had it?

'What's wrong, Kit?' Padding sleepily towards him, Nan could see the tears running in silent rivulets down a face which seemed suddenly old. The moon had turned his flesh to the colour of ice and his eyes to the hard glitter of sapphires. She stood looking up at a broken man.

'Come back to bed, Love. Tell me.' Raising a hand she carefully brushed a wayward tear from his cheek, just as he had once done for her all those years ago on Midsummer Meadow.

Kit looked down as though seeing her for the first time. Her soft curls were still warm and tousled from sleep; her eyes wide with worry. Bare feet peeped out from beneath the long, white flowing nightgown. A sob caught in his throat. Was this one really an angel, or were all women disciples of the devil? As he stood there, wondering, he felt her arms creep cautiously around his neck and the gentle pressure of her head resting on his shoulder. Her breath was sweet against his skin; the curving, feminine shapes of her body touching his, torturing him with agonized memories of the rude awakening he had suffered earlier. The act of stretching to kiss the base of his throat moved her breasts against his chest in a caressing motion.

Nan gasped at the sudden pain as his fingers dug into the flesh of her shoulders, thrusting her from him to hold her at arm's length.

'What do you want of me, Temptress? Do you tease me in order to shame me? Rouse me to laugh at me? Mock me behind my back?' His eyes were black with fury as pain turned to anger. She should be taught a lesson, and one which she would never forget. No woman would make a fool of Christopher Hatton again.

Lifting her bodily, Kit flung her across the bed, tearing the fine white linen from neck to hem as he did so. She lay there, terrified, clutching the ruined garment across her nakedness. With a growl more beast than man, the once-gentle lover, forced her, spreadeagle, to submit to punishing, undeserved rape. Again and again, until she was bruised and bleeding and too numb to even cry. Until he had taken revenge against the sly deceitfulness of women.

Only when birds chorused the dawn and he

was quite spent, did he take her roughly in his arms and kiss her with some of his former affection, but even then he saw no reason to be sorry. She would get over it. Or leave.

Nan rose to tend the more severe of her wounds and try to wash away the flagrant degradation she had endured. Dressed for the day's work, she stood beside the turmoil of the disordered bed and looked down on his sleeping form. Naked. Vulnerable. She could have killed him had she so desired. Instead, Mistress Hobson carefully covered him against draughts and kissed his brow without disturbing him. Whatever had happened the previous day had frustrated some great ambition. Turned his world upside down. Destroyed his peace of mind. Perhaps one day he would tell her, but whether he did or not, she would still be there, by his side, if he wanted her.

CHAPTER SEVEN

Drums, pipes and cymbals rattled out a finale as the actors stepped forward to take their bow. The watching members of the Court followed Elizabeth in her applause and Kit Hatton's lip curled derisively in a sardonic smile. Robert Dudley's players were going from strength to strength since the City

Council had abolished travelling actors. Known as 'The Earl of Leicester's Players', the tightly knit group were true Thespians, giants of the boards drawn from enthusiastic amateurs; mummers forced to give up a nomadic pattern of life and put down roots. Roots which had provided them with a stability they never desired, but which formed a firm foundation on which they could build. There was talk of a permanent theatre. James Burbage, their leader, was constantly suggesting sites, waving his arms around open spaces, visualizing a stage with entrances and an enclosed pit to accommodate the paying gawpers. James had energy enough for two, larger than life and every inch an actor.

'And yet,' Kit thought to himself, 'I could teach him a trick or two.' Not posturing before a crowd in fancy dress repeating a script. How much more difficult was it to live a lie? To ignore the real meaning behind Elizabeth's constant refusals to marry? To hide the sickening revulsion he now felt for her maid? He had discovered how imperfect the world was, but he had also realized that those who would succeed used its imperfections to advantage. And so he was polite to Mistress Fytton, and even more attentive to the Queen. Music for the dance began, finding Kit bowing over Her Majesty's hand before the first fanfare had subsided. Her dazzling smile would have made his heart flutter once, but now he recognized it as merely a part of the game she played. The flattery he gave her in return? All part of the game. But it was not the only game in progress, though the overwhelming rule of the other sport was to carry it out beneath Elizabeth's nose without being caught. The unrepentant virgin Queen demanded celibacy from certain members of the Court, and her temper, should this law be flouted, was not a thing to contemplate lightly.

Kit could feel Elizabeth Cavendish's adoring eyes on his back as he performed the intricate steps in time to the music. She had not the slightest hope of him returning the gesture. He was smiling at the Queen as though she was the only woman in the room. In the world! But later, he would keep their rendezvous. The child was ripe for seduction. And there was little enough time to perform the operation before she was whisked off to her marriage when she would be created Lady Lennox, poor girl. Wife to the brother of none other than the late and unlamented Henry Darnley! The least he could do was to give her a night she would be able to remember in her old age. A night of poignancy and passion. Sweet seventeen. He could hardly wait.

But wait he had to, for on that particular night other things took place which needed his immediate attention. Lord Robert had excused himself, leaving Kit to shoulder the full burden of keeping Her Majesty entertained, and

Douglass, that of jealous speculation. John Sheffield's widow seemed nervous and fidgety; out of sorts with everyone these days and glaring suspiciously at any woman under forty with whom Robert chose to pass the time of day. And no one was immune from her black looks.

It was as Kit was returning to the hall after relieving himself that he heard the screeching accusations of that waspish voice, replied to by the equally vehement tones of another female. The first virago would appear to be getting the best of the argument, whatever it was about, though the other was certainly putting up a good fight. Opening the door of the room from which the noise was emanating he was just in time to see the first blow struck. Frances Howard recoiled as the forceful slap across her face stung tears to her eyes. Her sister pounced on her, tearing at her hair and scratching ferociously at her eyes. Blood oozed, separate droplets in a straight line, from nail-torn skin which was already beginning to swell with bruising.

'Whore! My own sister!' Douglass was panting with her exertions as she continued to pummel Frances. The rain of blows had her opponent on her knees, her arms raised in an effort to protect her face from further damage.

'No! I swear I haven't . . . Ahh!'

A vicious twist on her hair had Frances crying.

Kit Hatton grasped Douglass round the waist from behind and before that young woman knew what was happening she was held twelve inches above the ground, kicking helplessly and quite at a loss to know who had interfered in something which didn't concern them.

'Are you completely mad, Mistress? May I put you down without fear of your commiting murder? Are you all right?' This last was to Frances who was sobbing helplessly on the floor. She nodded tremulously, wiping a smear of blood from her cheek.

'She thinks I have seduced Robert away from her. If only I could! The chance would be a fine thing in itself!' Some of Mistress Howard's fighting spirit was returning now that she had a champion. 'Is it my fault if she spends her nights alone? Perhaps if she looked to herself for the reasons . . .'

Tightening his muscles Kit managed to restrain the wriggling woman in his arms. 'Enough, you stupid woman. Can't you see that she will tear you to stew-meat with her bare hands if you can't be civil?' And serve you right too, he thought to himself. He'd noticed Frances was not at the end of the queue when it came to leaning on Robert's arm. And Douglass must have been under a terrible strain, not being able to tell the world that she was married to the man. Not that she was. But that was another story! She was wide of the mark, however, when she accused her sister of fornication with the Earl of Leicester. Robert had other fish to fry and was in all probability tucked up warm and cosy with Lettice, Lady Essex at Durham House right at that very moment. Making the most of her husband being abroad on the Queen's business! He couldn't help chuckling to himself. The tangles they got into with their womenfolk! And was the effort really worth it, when all was said and done? There was not much to choose between them, truth to tell, and it was often a case of: better the devil you know . . .

Not for Robert, however, and on this occasion it was left to Kit to sort out the mess and keep the sisters apart.

'Go and tidy yourself. Find Meg Clifford. She will have something to stop the swelling and keep tongues from wagging. And then send her here to me with a potion to calm our little hellcat before she tears me to shreds as well.'

Frances made good her escape; a mouse scurrying away from the claws of a lynx as it hissed and spat after her from the confines of Christopher Hatton's strong arms. The minute the door closed, leaving them alone, Kit placed Douglass firmly in a chair and stood before her, frowning, legs apart and arms folded across his chest.

'So, Mistress! Was it pure speculation? Or was there firm evidence to provoke you to such a shameful display?' He waited as the panting woman caught her breath, shaking his head at the state she had got herself into. Her once elegant coiffure had been reduced to a tangled mess and her face which had always been so pert and pretty appeared puffy and blotched. A flaky, sweat-moistened surface. And the seams of her gown were coming adrift, revealing the grubby linen of her undergarments. Who could blame Robert? Frances had been right. Lettice Knollys was a very beautiful lady and Douglass had only to study her own reflection to see that the remedy, if there was one, lay in her own hands.

Lady Sheffield's anger had subsided to leave her shaking with impotence. And fear! Kit saw the concealed panic.

'Where is Robert? I need him. And please don't lie to me! No one knows more about his comings and goings than you.' There was a challenge in her words.

'And since when, may I ask, had the Earl of Leicester been answerable to you for his actions? What possible right could you have to question his whereabouts?'

'My marriage lines!' The reply was sharp and defiant.

'Ah . . . Yes, of course.' Kit nodded thoughtfully. 'Well, I really don't know where he is at this very moment . . . but I do expect to see him on the morrow in the Council Chamber . . . There has been some upset for

Elizabeth, thanks to Catherine de Medici's ridiculous sense of humour, and we are to listen to the French Ambassador's excuses on Her Majesty's behalf. Robert is expected . . .' His voice tailed off. Then again, Robert might very well be otherwise engaged! Anyway, what was so hell-fire important that Douglass had to see him urgently? Pulling up a chair he decided to change his tactics and, turning on the charm, set about solving the mystery. The answer wasn't long in coming.

'I am with child.' Douglass swallowed nervously. 'And I feel it time to tell the Queen about our marriage. If I am to stay at Court . . . I can't keep it a secret much longer, but for these last three months my husband has been so busy.'

Kit could have kicked himself for being so short-sighted. That would account for the split gown. And the puffiness around the eyes. A lonely Douglass Sheffield had lately been in the habit of crying herself to sleep. But as for the marrige becoming common knowledge . . . 'I should step very warily in that direction if I were you.'

The young woman couldn't fail to hear the warning in Kit's voice. Why? What had Robert now to gain by silence? If Elizabeth ever did decide on marriage, and that would take a miracle, then it was no use the Earl of Leicester putting himself forward as a husband. He couldn't. He was already wed!

'Don't tread too forcefully on Robert's toes or you could easily find yourself put away.' Kit paused to let this sink in. 'All things are possible . . .'

Douglass looked at him doubtfully. 'Put away? In what manner?'

'You haven't forgotten, surely, how swiftly the doctors pronounced your first husband dead of natural causes? Robert has more men in his pay than anyone I know and he made sure that not a single shred of evidence was left to implicate you in any way.'

'To implicate me?' Douglass was shocked; unable to believe the unspoken accusation. 'I had no hand in John's death. No one could possibly have thought . . . No! It's a lie!' She had been madly in love with the handsome earl, but not enough to murder . . .

'Don't look so innocent.' Kit patted her hand. 'You must have known that Robert would find out? And that he would protect you?'

'Find out? Find out what?' Douglass had never questioned John's death too closely, not wishing to know the truth, and always having tucked up in the back of her mind that Robert had loved her enough to . . . to . . .

'What do women usually resort to in such circumstances? The sword? It was poison, as you very well know. And what can be covered up can be uncovered as easily, should the time be ripe.'

She stared, wide-eyed, at Christopher Hatton, a man she had always thought of as gentle. Lacking in ambition. Unforceful. Not like the rest of the Queen's courtiers who stabbed each other in the back regularly with little or no provocation. He had changed. The smooth, polished exterior was as charming and deferential as ever, but it now hid a heart which was becoming hardened to life at Elizabeth's Court; a heart of pure gold which was in the process of being transmuted into something indescribably base and as unyielding as granite. She would never have thought that he, of all people, could suggest that she had had the temerity to kill her own husband. And did Robert, as Kit had hinted, believe such a thing? If he did, what manner of men were these who could hide the evidence without a second thought and proceed to live with, and make love to, a woman they suspected of being a murderess? Would they themselves stop at removing a person who upset their plans? Douglass thought not. What in God's name was she to do?

Lord Robert had no doubts whatsoever about what must be done. Secretly, he had Tamworth search her rooms with orders that he seek out and destroy a certain folded parchment on which was written the date, time and place of a ceremony which supposed itself legal. The drunken witnesses, high-spirited in the aftermath of Lord Northampton's wedding, were friends whose loyalty was not in doubt, and so the lady could protest all she wanted. There was no evidence on earth to substantiate her ridiculous claims that she was the wife of the Queen's favourite. And woe betide her if she so much as tried! Arrangements were made that she retired to the country for rest and fresh air after a debilitating bout of sickness. She would be as right as rain when Elizabeth returned from her summer progress to Gloucestershire.

Had Robert Dudley only known it, this was but the start of a year which was to be given over to nothing but the troubles caused by the women in his life. Troubles which his friend and fellow courtier, Kit Hatton, would not entirely escape.

So far as the Queen was concerned, the progress to Bristol, which had been postponed from the previous year, was a great success, with the west of England opening its hunting grounds and its hearts to her. She listened with enthusiasm to the well-learned speeches of her subjects on every village green and cross road. She rode and she danced and she feasted. There was cock-fighting and bear-baiting, jugglers, tumblers and fools. And many a colourful play was produced for her entertainment in the open air of a warm summer evening. And by her side, day and night, week after endless week, was the slim, flaxen-haired beauty, Elin von Snakenburg.

Lord Northampton had not survived his marriage long, much to the amusement of certain young men who swore that they too could die happy in the same circumstances, given half a chance. Mary Fytton did her best to remain cheerful and attentive, but she knew that she was fighting a losing battle. Elin's purity shone irreproachably from the summer-blue of her eyes. Despite her widowhood she was virginal. As virginal as the Virgin Queen could ever wish for. Chaste and unsullied.

Here was a novelty! It looked as though the dark-haired siren was losing her place to an angel in white. Kit watched the muted charade of jealousy and spite as it was acted out, unseen, beneath the noses of everyone in the company. To others it was simply a case of petulance brought on by the Queen making a fuss over a bereaved young woman, and childish under the circumstances. Only Kit saw a woman scorned. Eaten up by jealousy as she was replaced in her lover's heart and bed by tender youth. And he marvelled as Elizabeth kept the whole situation completely under control with a skill born of long years of practice. She had kept Kings and Heads of State at bay for years in the same way without things ever coming to blows, so the handling of two dependant maids posed no problems at all. In fact, she was enjoying it. He smiled to himself as he watched her. She should have been born a man, and no mistake! At that moment the Queen looked up and caught traces of amusement on his face. Raising a quizzical eyebrow she beckoned him to her side.

'Have I a smut on my nose, Mister Hatton? Or am I just comical?'

'Neither, Your Majesty. I was admiring your outstanding brilliance. Though surrounded by beauty on all sides,' he indicated the dark and the fair, both remaining determinedly close to Elizabeth's chair, 'Yet you have no trouble in outshining them all.'

A sudden sharp twinge brought a flicker of pain to his eyes. The Queen was quick to notice.

'You are unwell? Pray, tell me.'

Kit blushed uncomfortably. He had been suffering this same illness, off and on, for many years, but lately had found it more than a slight nuisance. It had become downright painful and inconvenient. And it was a delicate subject. An infirmity which had him pissing every five minutes, the execution of which act forced him to bite back groans as the hot, yellow liquid stung like vinegar in an open wound. What brought the attacks on he couldn't tell, and they only seemed to subside in their own good time. The Queen would not let the matter drop until she had the truth of it and a worried frown creased her brow.

'Perhaps you should take the waters. Would that help, do you think? I shall ask the doctors their opinion, and though it will break my heart to let you go, for the good of your health I must manage without you.'

She had enough to keep her happy and occupied with Elin, Kit knew. Like a child with a brand new puppy to train; teaching it to jump at her every command. And it wasn't many days later when he realized that he had a ready-made excuse for leaving the progress to attend to other business.

Will Clewer, one of Robert's men left behind to keep an eye open for information, rode into the village beyond the Salisbury Plain as though the devil had his tail. The news he whispered to the Earl of Leicester privately had Robert reaching for the wine, though whether in celebration or for fortification Kit was not sure. Douglass Sheffield had been brought to bed of a son!

In the seclusion of a reserved room, in an inn tucked cosily in the lea of St. Catherine's Hill, and well away from the ears of Elizabeth's entourage, two of her favourite men opened a second bottle. Through the window Kit absently watched a brace of plovers take to the air above the neighbouring woods. Would that men could fly from their responsibilities so easily!

'What are you going to do?'

'Get rid of it, I hope.' It was a flat and unemotional statement. 'Dear Lord! A man's body plays some foul tricks on him!'

'And isn't that the truth!' Kit agreed with him wholeheartedly, still painfully aware of his noxious, pestilential member.

'All these years I have whored without fear or favour and so far as I know, never fathered a single child. Yet by the same messenger I hear that Douglass has my lusty son sucking hungrily at her paps, and that Lettice is convinced she will be in similar plight before next spring. The first I can find a way out of, so long as I keep the Queen sweet and let the lad grow a little before his existence comes to her notice. But this other! By Walter Devereux's wife! And whilst he is away on the Queen's business!'

Kit couldn't help grinning at him ruefully.

'Don't look at me like that.' Robert managed a wry smile. 'You once told me that I was welcome to all the ladies of the Court and that you would stay with the ladies of easy virtue. Perhaps you were right after all.'

His friend shook his head. 'Perhaps if we had controlled our urges and lived more prudently I would still be able to cross my legs in comfort and you would not be scouring the land for midwives!'

'Ah, but come now! Wasn't it worth it?' Robert slapped him companionably on the back. The wine was beginning to have the desired effect. 'Remember the Penny twins? Remember the woods at Belvoir . . . Oh no. You weren't in the woods that night, were you?'

'No. I was covering your tracks for you. As usual.' Kit did, however, have other memories. Some of which Robert hadn't even heard about.

'Aye. There are times when we need our friends. Now, for example.'

A plan was beginning to ferment. The Earl was renowned for his perspicacity and level-headedness. Especially in tight corners.

'It isn't a midwife I require. I need . . . I need Meg Clifford.'

So that was what he meant by get rid of it! Kit had a fleeting vision of a once-vibrant gipsy girl, sitting bruised and tearful in a small thicket, a bunch of wilted herbs in her hand. A soft, warm human being. There were no such females around the Court of Elizabeth, and Lady Essex would have no qualms whatsoever about taking the step a ragged tinker's daughter had balked at.

'But how?'

The practical details brought Kit back to the present. Then suddenly he knew.

'Elizabeth has been worried about my ailment and only the other day suggested that I leave the progress to take the waters. How do you feel? I could use some company for a week or two if you thought that the same treatment would improve your health. And you could always offer to bring some of the magic liquid back for Her Majesty's own refreshment.'

'Excellent! I shall send Tamworth to Meg immediately. He won't argue with those orders!' Robert winked. He knew very well of the long-standing arrangement which kept both his body servant and the Queen's distant cousin happy. 'And we shall be away within the week.'

There was very little going on around the Queen which did not come to the attention of Mary Fytton sooner or later and the arrival of Clewer, followed shortly afterwards by the departure of Tamworth, was worth investigating. Something was afoot! Something involving Robert which was being kept from Elizabeth. What? Another woman? As it had been that time when Kit Hatton so successfully kept John Sheffield from bumping into his wife's lover? Mary tried desperately to swallow her bitterness. All she had achieved in that instance was making the woman available for him. Hate burned inside her. Hate for the sly deceitfulness of men. And women! Women like Elin. The Queen's new toy. She spat into the rushes, her fingernails digging into the palms of her hands as she tried by physical means to overcome the mental anguish. She was alone. Deserted. Rejected. Why? Why didn't one single person in the whole of the universe love her?

It would have been useless to remind her of the countless times she had rejected others; of the way she had condemned all men for the faults of one. Or of how she had used her own body in an attempt to achieve an equality with Robert, a physical parity which anyone less vulnerable would have realized was a total impossibility. And she had failed. Even in that. Elizabeth's and Robert's halcyon, honeymoon days were over and they were now more like affectionate, long-standing friends than lovers. Husband and wife without the union ever being consummated. Without Robert ever becoming King! But without Mary Fytton becoming indispensable either.

Kit and Robert obtained the permission needed to leave the progress, on the understanding that they returned to Elizabeth's side the moment that Kit was cured. Robert was to return before that if possible. What the two didn't know was that within a few hours of them riding out, Mary Fytton was also asking to be allowed leave. To visit her old nurse at Littlecote Manor, which was no more than a ride from where the Court was at present resting. But the only view that old manor had of Mary was her back, disappearing down the road towards London.

*　　*　　*

The sight of Mortlake Church peering at her over the treetops brought Meg Clifford out of her daydream and reminded her that she was not simply out on a joyride. Studying the graceful figure of Lord Robert, stouter now, and with his hair turning to steely grey, she could well understand how women from all walks of life were willing to risk their reputations for an hour alone with him. He had a dignity which maturity had only added to, and a face on which age had chiselled character. Character which the ladies of the Court found fascinating. Irresistible. And still unmarried! A fact which was possibly part of the attraction. Briefly Meg thought of her own husband. Pompous and ineffectual. Always twittering on to no great effect. Or maybe that was simply her own jaundiced view of him as the marriage had been largely political, and arranged, rather than a love match. For a passion and excitement well within her reach she had never needed to look further than Lord Robert's body servant. Tamworth rode beside his master. Straight and strong. Handsome and ceaselessly untiring. And loyal. Meg's smile was a little smug as she considered the meaning of that word. Loyal. Between them they could turn the Earl of Leicester's world inside out, if they had a mind to. Not that they would ever be fool enough to try, having seen the sorry state some of that man's enemies had been brought to. There wasn't one man or woman in Robert's pay who would dream of stepping out of line, valuing their freedom and their lives too greatly to become turncoats.

A million sparks of sunlight glinting on the ripples of the Thames were doused simultaneously as a cloud passed over the sun, leaving the water grey and flat, and Tamworth sprang down from his horse. They had arrived. Meg glanced at the house of mellow brick, separated from the church by nothing more substantial than a swathe of well-tended grass and a wall dwarfed by regiments of hollyhocks in bright dress-uniform. Purples, reds and pinks. It all looked so . . . so pleasant. Pleasant and ordinary, on the outside. Not the kind of place you would guess at harbouring a mystic. An alchemist. A seer! Her lover, his hands firm on her waist, lifted her from her mount, and together the three entered the residence of Doctor Dee.

'Welcome, welcome!' The benign, fatherly figure held out both arms in a fulsome gesture. 'This is a delightful surprise. Susan!'

The doctor had only recently embarked on the perilous journey into matrimony and Meg was curious to see what kind of woman had been brave enough to throw in her lot with such an unusual partner. She might have expected unconventionality, or even a goodly measure of eccentricity, but Lady Strange had not prepared herself for the bizarre. Susan Dee answered the call of her husband almost immediately and Meg was acutely conscious that she was staring. So too were her companions. Before them stood one of the prettiest, most feminine creatures any of then had ever seen. In miniature! A mannikin. A perfect pink and white china-doll face topped by a mop of golden curls, and the curving figure of a full-grown woman, perfectly in proportion, on a body scarcely tall enough to do justice to a child of eight.

By his broad smile it was clear that John Dee enjoyed springing his little surprise on visitors and when, after the introductions, he sent her off to provide his guests with refreshment, he turned to Robert, waiting for an opinion. It wasn't long in coming.

'Beautiful!' The word was a sigh of envy. 'Where did you find such an exquisite creature? And are there any more where she came from?'

John tapped the side of his not inconsiderable nose. 'My talents are my calling-card and consequently I find myself admitted into all kinds of situations, and all manner of residences. You'd be amazed at the things some households hide away from the world. Frightened of cruel accusations and ashamed that they were the onces to produce freaks and oddities whilst the rest of mankind, in its lofty normality, sneers at them. And they expect me to resolve all their problems overnight.'

'And in this case, you did!' Robert grinned.

'Most willingly!' As they spoke the doctor

led them through into his library; a room so cluttered that it almost defied description. Every surface seemed to be covered with maps and charts, and around the walls were shelves containing more books than Meg had ever set eyes on in her life. There must have been thousands of them! All shapes and sizes. Surely the biggest library in the world! Added to this there were statues and globes and strange glass shapes whose purpose she couldn't even guess at. Three mechanical birds, an owl, a raven and a jay, glowered menacingly from one side of the room, four times life-size and a hundred times more ugly. When set in motion they produced a noise guaranteed to scare the most determined thief. And in a murky corner crouched an apparatus which looked as though it was capable of raising the devil himself. Meg had never seen a contraption designed to be used for the distillation of eggshells, which as everyone knows, is the only sure way of calming the fury of a storm, either on land or at sea.

From the centre of this jumbled medley a slim, young man rose politely as they entered; distracted from the signs and symbols scrawled across a yellowing map.

'Ah, yes. Allow me to introduce one of our intrepid explorers. A man who shares with me the belief that there is a fortune waiting to be picked up from distant shores, by those willing to venture forth. May I present Martin

Frobisher.'

It appeared that Mister Frobisher had hopes of furnishing himself with a ship, which, if his grand ideas were realized, would return to England loaded to the gunnels with gold, and he and John Dee had spent the best part of a fortnight studying the doctor's latest cartographic efforts. And the portents! The best maps in the world would be less than useless if the entrails of a rabbit predicted disaster. Robert was soon immersed in all the whys and wherefores of as yet unnavigated waterways, the reason for his visit forgotten, for the moment. He'd made a fortune once before on a similar expedition so the whole thing would bear looking into. And perhaps Kit Hatton would like to know the details!

It was only after the refreshments were finished and Martin Frobisher had finally departed that the real business of the day came under discussion. It was a very delicate matter. Money changed hands. A very delicate matter. Doctor Dee was used to such secrecy, as the size of his extensive, and very expensive library testified. Meg Clifford gave them the benefit of her experience. She had examined the lady in question and in her honest opinion, the child had been in the womb for about three months. Fourteen weeks at most. And she had in her possession all the necessary ingredients to resolve the problem. The only stumbling-block was the divination of the auspices. When would the gods show favour? And when would they frown?

The lady, John Dee understood, was one of great importance. So important that no one must even suspect her straitened circumstances. And far too important to be allowed to die in the execution of the operation. He nodded his head sagely as he lit the scented powder in the crucible. A circle must be drawn. The glass uncovered. And the most propitious time revealed.

* * *

Mary Fytton seemed to have drawn a blank. She could have sworn that Robert and Kit would have headed towards the capital, yet she had scoured their usual haunts without a single sighting. No one in London had seen them for weeks.

'They're with Her Majesty. On the progress.'

That was the only answer she got, for all her questions. They hadn't really gone to take the waters? Had they? No! Secret messages, carried post-haste, meant more than a mild infirmity. Kit Hatton's suppurating bladder had been nothing more than an excuse. Mary was sure of it. But the pair of them were certainly lying low, so whatever was afoot must be of great importance. To one or other of them. Or both! Then, quite by a stroke of good luck, she had her suspicions confirmed.

It was about two of the clock and Mary, wearing the drabbest of her day clothes to avoid attention, strolled nonchalantly through the streets past the ale-houses most frequented by Kit Hatton's clique in the hope of being able to substantiate her intuitions. The playhouse performances usually began at three so those hoping to watch should be making their way to the South Bank at any moment. The streets were almost empty of people of substance who were no doubt still digesting their dinners. Only the riffraff laughed and grumbled its way around; young men inciting each other to riot, taunting scholars on their way to school; children squabbling over the ownership of a wooden top; and a worried goodwife in her homespun gown carrying her husband's dinner to him in the Clink. Pimps and cutthroats and beggars in rags, and rufflers in their tawdry finery, the brains behind the petty criminals, all began to emerge from rat holes to add their contribution to city life. A young girl, scuttering along at top speed, head down and lost in her own thoughts, almost knocked Mary from her feet.

'Beg pardon, Mam.' The girl looked up, startled as Mary caught hold of her arm.

'Aren't you in Lady Sheffield's household?' Mary had a good eye for faces. 'Why all the hurry? Is it an errand of mercy which has you running on such a hot afternoon?'

By the guarded look on Magdalen Frodsham's face she could see that she was not far wide of the mark.

'Your mistress is not ill? Indisposed? Is there anything I can do to help?'

The poor girl didn't know what to do. Mistress Fytton was a great friend of the Queen . . . But then again, so was Lord Robert. And that didn't stop him from being a friend of Mistress Sheffield. Did it? A very close friend indeed. And Magdalen had a problem which had been worrying her all day.

Mary saw at a glance that the maid, a leggy, overgrown child, had been almost overlooked when brains were being given out. It wasn't long before she was listening to the whole tale, as Magdalen saw it. Douglass Sheffield had given birth to a boy and Robert's man had ridden through the night to take the joyous news to him. No one, least of all Mistress Sheffield, had expected him to leave the Queen's side, Her Majesty being quite unaware of these events. So Magdalen had stared in amazement to see none other than the Earl of Leicester himself leaving the grounds of Durham House.

Durham House! Robert's old town mansion! Now in the possession of Lettice Knollys, Lady Essex.

'So do I tell my mistress that his lordship is in town, for he hasn't made a move to call on her? Or even let her know that he is no longer with the Queen! I know she has been tormented by jealous thoughts and entertained ideas that he was deserting her even before she knew she was with child. He denied her accusations. He stayed with her some nights to put her mind at rest but we knew . . . We could see that our mistress no longer had the power to hold a man like that. And of course, the law allows even a married man to stray when his wife is big with child. And to go gallymooning afterwards.'

'And how is Lady Sheffield?'

'Recovering well, and in high hopes of travelling to meet the Queen's company when she is out of bed. Though whether she will find the man she will be looking for I cannot say.'

'Don't worry. Say nothing to your mistress. By the time she is well enough to travel Lord Robert will be back by the Queen's side and your lady none the wiser. He has not called on her for a very good reason. He is on the Queen's secret business and you would be as well keeping that piece of information to yourself. If you value your life!'

Magdalen was out of her depth. Value her life! Indeed she did! The ins and outs of intrigue at Elizabeth's Court were far outside her understanding. Nothing was ever as it seemed and the girl knew her limitations. She wouldn't say a word!

Discreet enquiries of the tradesmen calling

at Durham House gave every indication that her ladyship was not at home. Nor expected to be so for some days to come. The mystery deepened and Mary decided to make her way eastward along the Strand for an answer to the riddle. There had to be something in this subterfuge which she could use for her own ends. Some piece of information which would have the Queen praising her. Noticing her. And pushing dear little Lady Northampton into the background where she belonged.

Emerging from the filth and mire of London's overcrowded streets Mary strolled some way into the open countryside to think about her situation. Stopping beside a crystal stream she slaked her thirst gratefully before leaning against the twisted trunk of a stooping witchen tree. So Douglass Sheffield had been brought to bed of a son. Lord Robert's son! That news in itself would be enough to hurt Elizabeth. To bring caustic remarks raining down on the father. But there was more. Mary was sure of it. Involving Lady Essex. Closing her eyes she pictured Lettice Knollys in her mind. Vivacious. Flirtatious. And beautiful. In addition to all that she was also the Queen's cousin, which, if Robert really was playing fast and loose with another man's wife, made this particular game somewhat dangerous. Even if she was to become a widow the Queen would never allow any such liaison. She was totally possessive where that man was concerned, and though she herself would never marry him, jealousy would tear her apart if he was to take another woman to his heart. It was far, far worse than simply taking one to his bed. Douglass would ultimately be forgiven. But Walter Devereux's wife was quite another matter. Mary knew exactly how Elizabeth would feel to find out that she had been betrayed. Lost! Bereft!

Hot tears of humiliation squeezed themselves from under her lids as she visualized the scene again. The Queen's hand on Elin's waist as she presented the pretty pearl pendant. The wide blue eyes, overflowing with innocence and full of gratitude. And Mary virtually ignored when it came time for the Queen's toilet. She had heard nothing but her own heart pounding in her ears; felt her limbs tremble with the pain and anger of frustration. There had been nothing she could do. Nothing she could say. Unless . . . If Lord Robert was aiming high . . . And if she told him that her name was not really Mistress Fytton . . . And after all, the Queen could not forget overnight the hours she had spent with Mary . . . The hours she had spent with Robert! If only she could go through with it! How sweet would be her revenge! But . . . Robert was a man. Mary shuddered in the heat. Would she be able to cast that particular devil out? Overcome the brutal initiation suffered at the hands of

Mister Darrel? She had to! To arouse the Queen's jealousy. To make her forget her snow queen.

Every smile the Queen had bestowed on the child had been a knife-thrust in Mary's heart. Every gift and favour had been a personal slight. The dreadful soul-destroying pain of rejection twisted the normal reasoning of her mind until she was willing to become a party to any mad scheme, no matter how lunatic or demented. All she wanted to do was destroy; tear the hopes and happiness of others to shreds as hers had been. But in madness, Mary was not given to hysteria. Her unbalanced mind took refuge in cold, calculating insanity. Concealing herself behind the ornamental wall outside Leicester House she watched dispassionately as Meg Clifford held a hurried conversation with Tamworth, nodding repeatedly towards the topmost rooms of the battlemented tower. Was that where Robert was keeping his lover's tryst with Lady Essex? But the meeting had taken such secret arrangements . . . No. It had to be more than that! But what?

The sun set over the city in a blaze of crimson and orange glory, outlining the tallest buildings with a fiery halo, setting them alight in a last burst of energy before daylight finally died. And Mary felt suddenly vulnerable. The streets of London were not the ideal place for a young woman alone after dark, but she was not going to give up, come what may. Even if her lunacy ended in self-destruction. However . . . Tucking her skirts up inside her girdle, Mary pulled her cloak around her. Who, in the rapidly descending darkness would not take her for some young rake off to take his pleasure in the nearby Stews? It wasn't the first time she had resorted to such a disguise, and she had remained quite undiscovered in the matter of John Sheffield's death.

Twilight turned gradually to the pitch-black of night as the minutes slid by, damp river air chilling her as she stood stock still. Waiting. Numbness set in, every minute seeming like an hour, and an hour being long enough to cover the memories of a lifetime. Her stomach sounded like an empty drum as she swayed, light-headed with hunger, against the rough wall. It was going to be an endless night. And what did she hope to discover? Only instinct told her to stay. That, and thoughts of what Elizabeth was doing right at that very moment. Imagination became the cruellest weapon of self-torture, her heart mocking her with every unloved beat. The Queen had a new love to oil her body and tend her every need. And Robert? What was he indulging in? The faint light glimmering from the tower room drew her eyes. For years she had studied the man. From every angle. Fantasized about the hours he had spent alone with her mistress. Feared him. As a rival and as a man. That thought brought a bitter smile to her lips. And Robert had apparently had more women than there were stars in the heavens! He had taken the Queen for a fool, professing a love for her and her alone! Or had he? When all was said and done, only Mary stood alone!

A sudden sound made her start and catch her breath, turning to peer through the gloom. Two pairs of sinister green eyes watched her silently. Letting the air sigh from her lungs Mary reached out to stroke an inquisitive cat as it paused in its nightly patrol of the walls and rooftops of the city. Its sparse, mangy fur grey in the moonlight, blazed with lighter markings on head and chest. As though it had dribbled honey onto its coat.

Then everything happened at once. Footsteps, none too steady, were approaching, and Mary shrank back against the wall, making herself almost invisible. Whoever it was, they were the worse for drink! Then she let out a scream. From beside the gatepost rose a silent figure. A spectre. A ghost. All she could see was the whites of his eyes as he made a lunge for her. Had he been crouching in the darkness, watching her? And for how long?

In fact, the unhappy wretch had been sleeping off a bellyful of ale, and he had been more startled than Mary to find what for all the world appeared to be a likely young gentleman rubbing up against him. And some of the rich Court debauchees paid well for such services as he was willing to provide!

'What? Hold! Come out and show yourselves!'

Mary knew that voice. And realized her dilemma. As Kit Hatton drew his sword she felt the stinking vagrant's hand fumbling at her thighs. Rape? Or discovery? She turned to run. Then lamplight from the doorway of the house spilled out, capturing her in its exaggerated brightness like a frightened rabbit. And beside her, two men fought to the death.

Steel clashed with steel. The courtier's short sword had the advantage over a vagabond's dagger, but both were expert with their weapons, one having spent hour after hour practising his sport, and the other having had a lifetime's practice fighting for his life. Different techniques. Equal determination. The dagger ripped uselessly through the air as Kit sidestepped, thrusting at the crouching figure as he did so. The man circled slowly, knees bent, head forward, every muscle taut and ready to spring. This pastime wasn't new to him, as the livid scar mutilating one side of his face, showed. By his clothes, such as they were, he had been a sailor at some time. But not lately. Not since he had returned from that fateful expedition under Captain Hawkins, hardly any life left in him, and disfigured by a bastard Spaniard's sword. Shifting the position of his weapon, never moving his eyes from his adversary, he inched his way round, crab-like.

The light now fell on the unmarked side of his head.

'Robert! Robert Winchcombe!' Mary had spoken without realizing it. The years melted away and she was once more at Littlecote Manor. Choking on the dirt of the barn floor. Being sadistically raped by the perverted master of the house. As Robert Winchcombe looked on without lifting a finger to help her.

The squalid wreck of that once handsome youth paused. Lost his concentration for a fraction of a second. But it was enough. Kit's sword plunged into the soft part of his belly, slitting it apart before jerking free.

'Mary!' Was she real? Or an angel come to guide him?

He slumped to his knees, blood and entrails glossing a patch of the Earl of Leicester's lawn as he fell.

'Mary! Forgive me!'

She turned her head away, sickened by the sight of what he had become. Robert never knew. He had breathed his last. Mary held out her hand to Kit in a gesture of gratitude but to her dismay it was brusquely brushed aside.

'I would have done the same for anyone, Mistress. And he provided me with an excuse to settle a score. It was scurvy wretches like that who lost me a fortune and piled debts on my head which I fear will be the death of me, in the end. Never thank me for what was not intended.'

Mary recoiled as though he had slapped her. Kit Hatton too! The one man who had been unswerving in his devotion to her. No matter how she teased or insulted him. Now he had joined the ranks of the indifferent. Staggering slightly, Mary felt as though she was about to swoon. How long had it been since she had eaten? How long standing in the chill night air? And now this!

Then a firm arm round her waist held her steady and she smelt the familiar scent of his clothes and skin. Animal scents which she had sniffed out and savoured, secretly, around the Queen's private chambers. Robert Dudley scooped her up into his arms before she fainted clean away.

'Kit? You're not hurt?'

'Not at all. And quite sober into the bargain. I'd been out on . . .' He paused, realizing that there were women present. 'On the usual business . . . when for some reason I decided to find out how your problems were being resolved . . . thinking I might be of assistance . . .'

'And it seems that you were! Who is this fellow? And what in God's name was he doing near my house?'

'Best ask the trollop in your arms!' Kit's tone was derisory. 'She knew his name, unhappily for him. Had she not it might easily have been a different ending to his story.' If by any chance the Queen's favourite dancing partner had been murdered, the victim would certainly have been hung, drawn and quartered, making a name for himself into the bargain. As it was, he would simply disappear.

Robert looked thoughtfully at Mary, clinging now to his neck as though it was a lifeline. The slight nod of his head in Kit's direction was almost imperceptible. He would have the truth out of her before the night was over. But in the meantime, there were other more urgent matters to be attended to.

'Tamworth was to row out onto the river to dispose of . . . of that.' All eyes were on the bloody bundle held precariously in Meg Clifford's shaking hands. She had been wrong in her estimation, and the child, forced painfully and mercilessly into a world it was not ready for, had whimpered and cried piteously for endless minutes before she had plucked up the courage to smother it.

'And then he was to take Meg to Wanstead for the night, to rest before making the journey back to her husband's estates where it was planned that she would . . . er . . . rest for some considerable time.' Lie low, in other words. Well out of the way of Lettice, who would not wish to be reminded of this night's work for many a month. 'But now,' Robert continued, 'there is this other matter to be disposed of too. And I have my hands full!'

'Two of us will make short work of it.' Tamworth nodded agreement at Kit's words.

'We'll have the body in the boat in no time.'

Meg gave a moan. She was shaking all over as though struck with the palsy, her mind as bloodstained as her hands, staring at the red-streaked linen in the flickering lantern light, before her eyes were once more mesmerized by the twisting grey and yellow convolutions of a dead man's guts spilling out like offal at the meat market.

'Quick, then. Lift him down to the river. Then come back.'

Both men were well muscled and without a sound they swung the remains of Robert Winchcombe unceremoniously onto the complaining timbers of the rowing-boat.

'And now that.' Tamworth knew exactly what was meant. Taking the small bundle from Lady Strange's hands he disappeared into the darkness and within moments the others heard the creaking of oars. He would have to row much further than they had anticipated. Lord Robert wanted no corpses washed up in his garden.

'So, Kit? Will you fall in with this plan and escort the lady in place of Tamworth? A horse has been made ready and she will ride up behind you, not being in a fit state to see to herself.'

'And the other?' Kit inclined his head towards the pale light showing in the windows of the tower-room.

'She will be well soon enough. A strong-spirited woman, it would take more than this to kill her, thank God! But go now, and we'll meet in three days' time in Wiltshire!'

Mary had listened to the exchange in silence, scarcely daring to breathe. Had they forgotten that she was there? Her mind was in a whirl as she tried to assimilate all the information with which she had been bombarded in the last few hectic minutes. Meg Clifford had procured an abortion for Lettice, Lady Essex on Robert's behalf; Robert Winchcombe had materialized out of thin air, carrying the past into the present to haunt her; and Kit Hatton had become as hard and ruthless as the next ambitious courtier. Tonight she had seen him in a different light; felt the unyielding iron within the velvet glove. And she had experienced a totally unexpected emotion. A twinge of regret that his eyes had lost completely that expression of abject devotion; of eternally unrequited love. Mary knew that she had never wanted him, but it was surprising how much it hurt to realize that she had lost the power to attract him. No. She didn't want him, but she wanted him to want her!

And the most difficult thing of all to accept was the fact that she was at that very moment held securely in Robert Dudley's arms and being carried out of the night and into the safety and comfort of Leicester House. The hunger and horror caught up with her, and she fainted.

CHAPTER EIGHT

On opening her eyes Mary hadn't the faintest idea where she was. The canopy above the bed on which she lay was of deep, rich purple, emblazoned with a device worked thickly and ornately in gold. The soft, downy pillows which cushioned her head shone with the sheen of silk; and a glowing crimson velvet cover nestled in rippling perfection around her inert form. The whole room, gently shadowed by firelight, was palatial, with tapestries adorning every wall and gilded chairs gleaming brightly in darkened corners. And on a carved oak table beside her bed shone a small crystal lamp so exquisite that it took her breath away. Around its central golden spindle were hung a multitude of glass droplets, each faceted to turn every glimmer of light into a miniature rainbow, scintillating brilliance with every subtle movement of the air.

'You like it?'

Mary started at the sound of his voice. She hadn't realized that she wasn't alone in the room, but there he was, leaning casually against the high chimney-piece as though he had just turned from studying the blazing logs. Embarrassed and tongue-tied, she tried to sit up, only to discover that when she did so dizziness again swept over her. In three strides he was by her side, sitting on the edge of the bed.

'Lie down and keep calm. Tamworth will shortly be bringing mulled wine and a bite to eat.'

At the mention of Tamworth's name the events of the evening came rushing back into her muddled mind and with a groan she covered her face with her hands.

'What time is it? How long have I been here?'

'Hush now. What does time matter? All that really matters is that we get you well.' Robert stroked the wayward curls from her brow in a gentle, caressing movement.

Mary began to shiver uncontrollably. Terrified. She was alone, in Leicester House, with Robert. Her rival. The one man on earth to have spent the night with Elizabeth Tudor; to have lain with her naked! Jealousy and fascination mingled. And now he was with her. Mary. Smiling at her. Touching her face. Concerned for her welfare. She closed her eyes.

The question Robert wanted answering was, why was she here in the first place? Had Elizabeth sent her to spy on him? It seemed an unlikely choice of agent, but what other reason could there be? Had the Queen not believed that he and Kit had travelled to take the waters? She was a devious woman and he could easily convince himself that she was capable of seeing through any of his ruses. Whatever the truth was, he would soon have it out of Mary. A special blend of Meg Clifford's spiced wine would begin the seduction, as it so often had. And he would finish it.

Tamworth left the room as silently as he had entered, knowing the value of discretion at a time like this. Word of the revolting events in which they had all played their parts must go no further, and no one was better qualified to prevent it spreading than Lord Robert. The woman would be clay in his hands.

'Come, now, Love. Drink this down. It will do you good.'

Mary lifted herself up on the pillows.

'Here. Let me help you.' Robert slipped his arm around her and raised the goblet to her lips. The hot liquid, headily aromatic, trickled soothingly into her stomach, warming her inwardly and bringing a becoming rosiness to her pale cheeks.

'Thank you.' Mary smiled at him wanly, gazing up into the darkest eyes, smouldering with passion, that any normal woman could wish to see.

'Mary.' He said the word as though it was a prayer. 'So lovely. So precious.'

The shocked, uncontrollable trembling of her limbs began again. Painful memories of brutality and violence lurked menacingly at the back of her mind.

'You're cold.' Robert eased himself onto the

bed to lie beside her, his arms encircling her; holding her close.

Mary shook her head. 'No . . . Not cold.'

'Not frightened, surely?' His mouth was only inches away from hers. She could feel his breath on her lips; see her own petrified reflection in his eyes. 'There's nothing to be afraid of. After the vile impertinence of that ruffian I only wish to take care of you . . . I won't hurt you. See.' Closing the gap betwen them he softly brushed her mouth with his. 'That didn't hurt, did it?'

It was the first time a man had kissed her without a fight, and the gentleness surprised her. A kiss as soft as . . . And as tender.

He felt her relax a little. 'You knew that wretched sailor's name?' He kept his voice to a whisper so as not to panic her.

Mary nodded, but as yet, could not bring herself to speak. She was facing more immediate worries as the sick horror of Mister Winchcombe's death was swamped by fear of Robert Dudley's reputation.

'How?' Robert was not going to let the matter drop. He kissed her again, letting his hands stray unobtrusively to calm her palpitating breast. 'I have known you for . . . how long? Yet I know so little. Now you can tell me everything. Absolutely everything.' The ties of her dress unravelled themselves under the guidance of his skilful fingers and Mary froze, rigid and unco-operative as his hand came into contact with her naked flesh for the first time. Only biting her bottom lip until she could taste the salt blood on her tongue prevented her from pleading with him to stop. She didn't want him to stop. Tears of frustration, tears of impotence, ran in unrestrained floods as she fought a frantic battle with her emotions. Then, as Robert murmured soothing noises into her ear and licked the tears from her face, lulling her fears, calming her nerves, the whole sordid story was at last torn from somewhere deep within her. A festering pustule which was finally being lanced.

It had all begun when Mistress Fytton took the young Mary into Winchester to see the Queen ride by. Queen Mary, that was. But she had been made to swear on her mother's bible that she would never renounce the New Faith, or make herself known to the papist Queen or any of her Court.

'Why?' Robert wondered quietly, out loud.

'Mistress Fytton was worried that I might be used by unscrupulous people to further their cause, and that I would end as my father had done.'

'Your father?' He kissed her brow in an almost fatherly way, although the fingers pinching provocatively at her proud, uptilted nipples were anything but fatherly.

'My . . . my father was Thomas Seymour. King Henry's brother-in-law. King Edward's uncle. Queen Katherine Parr's fourth and final husband.'

Robert kept quite still in case any movement stopped the flow of words. 'So your mother . . .?'

'Queen Katherine! Almost a princess. I was almost a princess. And Elizabeth Fytton took it upon herself to hide me in the country. A kitchen maid. That's all I was. Until the day she told me of my parentage and I knew. I knew that I was not destined to remain in the servants's quarters for ever.' Mary almost choked on a sob and Robert tightened his grip, holding her close to him.

Well, well! This was an unexpected bonus! Tom Seymour's daughter. No wonder the Queen had kept her close. Robert remembered well those youthful days spent at Chelsea Palace under Katherine Parr's motherly protection, in company with the young Elizabeth Tudor. Katherine had been heavy with child when her husband, Tom, had seduced the Princess Elizabeth under his wife's roof. Elizabeth had cried her heart out when Katherine sent her away, so in love with the lecherous Tom had she been. And in the end his ambitious scheming had brought him to the block. Beheaded for treason! And his wife had died in childbirth. Robert looked down at the trembling girl in his arms. Thomas Seymour's daughter! Katherine Parr's daughter! He couldn't believe it.

'The kitchen was no place for me, was it?' Mary was begging him to agree with her.

'No, of course it wasn't. Unthinkable! But how did you come then to Court?'

Mary Seymour, as he now knew her true name to be, turned her face into his shoulder, shuddering with revulsion at the memories.

'I . . . I thought to better my position by becoming the mistress of that house, but I hideously misjudged the master's intentions towards me. I thought he was so interested in his stables . . .' She broke off to wipe her nose and sniff back tears. 'How could a child have known such things as . . .'

'As what? You can tell me, Sweetheart.' His voice was low and husky.

Mary gazed up trustingly into his eyes. Yes. She could tell Robert. He was like no other man on earth.

'He . . .' She swallowed hard and then tried again. 'His interest lay solely with Nathan. His groom. A handsome youth who would do anything the master wanted at any time of the day or night. Sweet Nathan, everyone called him, behind his back, though that meant nothing to me at the time. I only knew that the master was not married, and that if he was to take a wife, then she would be a lady of substance who could command the scullery maids and eat off the high table. Until that terrible day when he took me into the old barn . . .' Her eyes were wide with remembered horror. 'Face down on the earth, my skirts thrown over my head . . . and then . . .'

Robert felt the rigidity of her body as she relived that perverted rape. As she fought against the awful agony . . . 'All right. Hush now. I understand.' He rocked her gently in his arms as though she was still that violated child. 'Don't think about it. It was a long time ago, and not all men are so brutal. Are they?' He smiled down at her reassuringly.

Mary shook her head. 'I don't think so . . . but the truth is that I don't know. Robert Winchcombe lived in that house too, his mother being a friend of my old nurse, and he professed to love me. Yet he stood in the barn that day and watched . . . without lifting a finger to help me . . .'

'Ah, but how old was he? And how strong against his employer? And could he jeopardize his mother's position in the household? For all you know, you could have been the very reason for him running away to sea. And judging by his scars, his had not been an easy passage either.' Certain things were beginning to make sense. No wonder Elizabeth had kept the girl at her side without ever offering her in marriage. If Mary had inherited one fraction of her father's ambition, given an equally ambitious husband . . . But there had been this other obstacle in the way of that, as Kit Hatton had proved. For all his overtures, his gifts and his pleas, she had held him off, even though

Kit was handsome enough to be sought after by at least half the beauties of the Court. The Queen chose to believe that he remained unmarried out of love for her, but Mister Hatton was too astute to tread on Robert Dudley's toes by seriously considering any relationship with Her Majesty which would take him beyond the bounds of propriety. All of which indicated that Mary was still a virgin. Even Kit had finally given up the chase without ever bedding her. And here she was, in his arms, in an almost deserted house, at dead of night.

To give the man his due, he did pause to give a thought to the woman lying in the room above, bleeding and in pain after the induced premature birth of her child. But she would never know. Mary wouldn't dare to say a word for fear of Elizabeth. All his amorous exploits had to be handled discreetly, but this brief interlude was just the medicine he needed. What with one son in hiding and another at that moment making food for the fishes he deserved a little titillation to take his mind from the mess. And wouldn't he enjoy describing the event to Kit later!

Mary lay quiescent as his hands explored her body with a tenderness which allayed all her fears. He wasn't forcing her to do anything. He was using all his subtlety and experience to arouse her, slowly but inexorably, determined not to frighten her with these new sensations. But to his immense surprise, as he slid his hand between her thighs, her eyes widened with amazement. Amazement and absolute joy. Then she began to move against him in a way which was far from clumsy. She was the most accomplished virgin he had ever come across!

That first sensational thrill when he touched her, as gently as Elizabeth ever had, broke the ancient bonds with which she had been shackled. Mary rose to meet him in that familiar pulsing world of ecstasy, thought subdued by feeling, body overruling brain. And then for the first, and last, time in her life she responded instinctively to a man as a woman should. She knew strength without violence, dominance without aggression and a deep sense of sharing which she had thought incompatible with masculine superiority. He entered. He took her. And the whole complexion of the world changed. She would never be the same again. Thank God!

* * *

If Mary wore a smug, self-satisfied look in the weeks which followed the Queen was too occupied with affairs of state to notice it. And Elin put it down to a ploy to arouse interest and command attention from a maid whose star was descending. Elin had nothing to fear, and she knew it. But for Robert it was quite a different matter. He didn't want the stupid woman casting him surreptitious glances which were liable to be noticed by half the Court. Taking her aside he warned her, leaving her in no doubt that he would deny that anything improper had ever occurred between them. He had enough to cope with, Douglass nagging him to tell the Queen that she was his wife, and Lettice, now fully recovered, taking up more of his time than he had ever allowed a woman in his life. He hated to admit it, even to himself, but Lady Essex meant a lot to him. Too mature to make a complete fool of himself, he nonetheless found it difficult to put her out of his mind when they were apart. And he had just heard that Elizabeth had recalled Walter Devereux from Ireland to answer charges of incompetence. He was edgy and short-tempered and determined that Lettice's husband would favour England with his presence for as short a time as possible. He would see to it that the charges were squashed. Answered in full and dismissed. The thought of that lovely woman cohabiting with Essex made his blood boil. Yet the man had a husband's rights in the matter and even the Earl of Leicester could do nothing about that. Yet!

As the golden days of October faded to the damp, fog-filled miseries of November Mary made herself scarce. Elation had given way to despair as the truth slowly dawned on her.

That glorious moment of revelation, that mysterious blending of two souls, man and woman, had been a lie. As Elizabeth's had. As Kit Hatton's had. The whole world was fickle. And she was left with results of that fleeting passion. With child! Hiding the morning vomits was bad enough. But how was she going to disguise a thickening waist? If Elin fell from favour and Elizabeth looked again at Mary, her faithful maid for many years . . . It didn't bear thinking about! Nor could she forget the pathetic, bloodstained bundle in the trembling hands of Meg Clifford on the night it had all happened. Meg was still absent from the Court, far out of reach, even if she had been willing to perform the same service for Mary as she had for Lettice.

Numbing cold pierced her body as Mary prostrated herself before the altar of the church. All night she lay, trying to pray. Asking for guidance. For some way out of her lonely situation. There was no man she could turn to. Now there was only God.

'O consider mine adversity, and deliver me: for I do not forget Thy law. Avenge Thou my cause and deliver me . . .'

This was surely her darkest hour; a hopeless void through which she tumbled, weightlessly. Unloved. Unwanted. Cast aside by one and all. She cried then for the mother she had never known. For the father who had chased power to the exclusion of all else, including his infant daughter. And then, as dawn glimmered through the window, she remembered that one old woman had loved her. Had cared for her, albeit in the kitchen of a manor house. She had not wanted for food or clothing or a roof over her head, despite the fact that Elizabeth Fytton had herself been almost destitute at the time of Tom Seymour's death. Hadn't she promised Katherine Parr that she would care for the child until her dying breath? Did that promise still hold true? No one knew more about herbs and potions than Mistress Fytton, not even Meg Clifford! Was it possible . . .?

The Queen was sympathetic. She remembered the old woman well and had much to thank her for. Of course Mary could visit her. And take Elizabeth's good wishes with her. We all had to die, sooner or later and the woman must be past her seventieth year. It was understandable that Mary should wish to be with her as she passed into a better life than this world had offered her.

Mary hugged her cloak round her and set her face towards Littlecote Manor.

* * *

God's blood! Here was a tangled web and no mistake! And Kit Hatton found himself right in the middle of it as usual, through no fault of his own. Riding north on a glorious summer day washed fresh by an early morning shower, he saw nothing of the rolling meadows and game-packed forests as he entered the county of Warwickshire. Peasants' huts and half-timbered houses, their owners touching forelocks and raising caps, were left behind unnoticed and unacknowledged as Mister Hatton pondered on his problem. How much should he tell the Queen? How much did she already know? If only he had been able to talk to Robert before Elizabeth had decided to investigate the disappearance of her personal maid. And why, in God's name, had Robert brought about such an event? Ruthless? Aye! But this! Even Kit, knowing Robert as he did, had blanched when he heard the whole story from the mouth of Edith Winchcombe, the kitchen maid at Littlecote Manor. How could he possibly tell Elizabeth the tale, knowing that she and Mary . . . He remembered clearly the day of Norfolk's execution. He wished he didn't! But for the woman to end like that! And the child! No. He couldn't tell the Queen the whole truth or he would be answerable to Robert . . . and Robert had a way of dealing with problems which kept gravediggers in employment.

The dull red walls of Kenilworth intruded on the green of the landscape, its beauty reflected perfectly in the mirror smoothness of the artificial lake, endless windows vying with the water for sparkle in the July sun. Robert had improved the building beyond the bounds of possibility, and the Queen could not fail to be impressed either by the place itself, or by the lavish entertainment planned to fill her every waking hour. And Kit wished again that the news he bore was not all bad.

Elizabeth had indeed been in the best of spirits. For eleven days she had been treated to a great variety of diversions, with music and dancing, plays and tumblers, and the finest display of fireworks any of them could ever remember. And one evening there was a water pageant which surpassed all expectations, with a mermaid swimming alongside a dolphin, a delight not only to the nobility but to the people of the surrounding villages who had also been invited to attend. And then Kit arrived.

Elizabeth could tell from his face that she must expect the worst. Robert, standing behind her as she received her handsome courier, frowned a warning and indicated silence with a slight shake of his head. But Kit had to say something. Part of the truth at least, must be told.

'Come to me later, after you have supped and rested and we shall talk. I have missed you, Mister Hatton. Especially in the dance.'

There was not going to be time for Kit and Robert to discuss the matter first, the Earl having his time fully occupied in playing the attentive host at all times. And making sure that Lettice behaved herself in as unobtrusive a manner as possible. He was sure that the Queen had her suspicions. She was no one's fool! If Kit said one word too many on this other matter, then the whole of this enterprise and hospitality, designed to sweeten Elizabeth, would have been a complete waste. It would become a fiasco.

'You know?' The question was muttered under cover of general chatter.

Kit nodded. 'Aye. Everything.' His expression was non-committal. Vacant of either condemnation or approval. He was no longer the callow youth who had arrived at Court; innocent and willing to please. He had learnt the value of discretion. One couldn't survive long without it.

'And . . .?'

'There is no need for her to know everything, but I have to tell part of it. For all our sakes. Have your excuses ready. For Mary's retirement. The rest shall be an act of God and nothing more.'

Robert eyed him speculatively. Then he nodded. 'I'll make it right. I'll have my players form my excuses into a play, begging her pardon for my human frailty. She loves to forgive when I throw myself on her mercy, and it will certainly serve to take her suspicious mind from Lady Essex. But I am in your hands.'

Kit realized that his own future was also at stake. No matter how deep the disgrace

Robert fell into, it was always temporary. But others were not so lucky, and should his friend so ordain, Kit could easily find himself an outcast from the life he had learned to enjoy. From the ambitions which he had every hope of one day attaining. God willing.

'I'm sorry.' Kit dropped to one knee before the Queen and bent his head over her hand to brush the slim, white fingers with his lips. Even when the homage was complete he couldn't bring himself to look her in the eye until he had composed his thoughts.

'Kit?' Elizabeth's voice was gently insistent. 'Tell me? She is dead?'

Kit raised his head but kept his gaze on the great pearl-flanked emerald glittering in the hollow at the base of her throat, the brilliant blue of his eyes hooded; shielded from her questioning. He nodded.

'How?'

He didn't flinch. Not a single muscle twitched to indicate that he was about to lie, and for the first time since entering the room Kit looked directly into those piercing, violet eyes; those shrewd, all-seeing eyes.

'In childbirth.'

The flat, unemotional statement caused a perceptible hardening of Elizabeth's attitude. Had she not been expecting that? Obviously not. Death by accident; by the fever; by the flux. But never death by childbirth. Not Mary! Kit would dearly have loved to keep the information to himself. To keep Robert's name out of it. But that part had to be told, as he had soon realized. Sir Henry Knyvett had been nosing around; prying into certain events which had taken place in the Darrel household, and had already got the support of Lord Hertford in bringing it to the Queen's attention. She would have heard that evidence sooner or later. Better to hear it from Kit Hatton, Robert's friend, than from any other source.

'I hate to be the one to bring such news, Your Majesty. I know . . . I know how great a store you put on Mary's friendship . . .' Kit faltered over the words as the Queen fought conflicting emotions. Childbirth! The thing they had both dreaded! Or had they? Had Mary lied to her through all those years? Had she been making a fool of Elizabeth the whole time? Had she always had lovers? Sweating, heaving men? Had she only used her Queen's love to further her own ambitions? To be as close to the throne as . . . as Robert? Just as her father before her had tried . . . The Queen leaned back in her chair, blinking back the sting of tears which started at the memory of Tom Seymour. Like father, like daughter. Loving one for the other only to find herself betrayed again! It was as well the whore had died! It could have been an infinitely more humiliating end at the hands of a woman scorned!

'And the father of the child?'

Kit squirmed uncomfortably but made no reply.

'Ha! The truth is so distressing then? That narrows the field somewhat. Not you, is it, Kit?'

'Your Majesty!' Kit's head jerked back indignantly. 'I admit that in my youth I did admire Mary and made some play to get her attention, but she made it very clear to me that her life was dedicated to her monarch and that no humble squire could presume to come between her and her mistress . . .' He swallowed hard.

Elizabeth was staring at him intently. 'I mean . . .'

The Queen leaned forward until her face was only inches away from his. 'I think I know exactly what you mean, Mister Hatton.' The piercing pupils of her eyes, black pinpoints, dared him to turn away.

And Kit saw what the woman was made of. What fools they had been! How could they have thought for a moment that they had ever deceived her? Oh, she might not know every detail of every escapade they had embarked upon, but he was certain that she knew her men. Inside out! Better than they knew themselves. They had got away with nothing. Not Robert. Nor himself. Nor any other courtier. Like a benevolent parent she had been strict when necessary, encouraging them to use whatever skills God had given them, to the good of their country. And their Queen. And in return, they had been allowed a certain freedom. To play, and cheat, and think that they had fooled her. They should have known she would never marry. It would have meant selling her country short! And Elizabeth would never do that. And from this day on, Kit Hatton determined to throw in his lot with her. Come what may. In response, her lips brushed his in thanks for the loyalty she knew she could depend on.

'Permit me to reward a humble squire.'

Kit broke out in a sudden sweat. Was there a hidden promise in those few words? Or was his imagination working overtime?

'And the child?'

The moment had passed as though it had never happened and the Queen was once more in command.

'That too died.'

'Mmm . . .'

Was that a sigh of relief? For the fact that a problem had been removed? For the fact that the last tie binding her to Tom Seymour and her past had now been broken? Then her eyes narrowed as she considered the remaining small mystery in the whole sordid affair.

'The father? Need I ask?'

Their eyes met in a look of mutual understanding. How well they both knew and understood Robert. He had got himself into another mess. And got himself out of it! Kit still marvelled at the man's audacity, realizing that no matter how hard a man he might eventually become, he would never equal the Earl of Leicester when it came to controlling destiny. When it came to cold-blooded murder!

'Dear Kit. How do we deserve your devotion? The most faithful friend a man . . . or woman . . . could ever have. Where Robin is my Eyes, you are my Lids. Whatever secrets I have, I know they are safe with you. And your faithfulness and loyalty shall not go unrewarded. As for my other obedient servant . . . I think he should sweat a little before I forgive him.'

Christopher Hatton lost no time in finding Lord Robert, warning him that the Queen was preparing to make some show of displeasure, and making sure that the preparations for an apology were in hand. They were. The play was already written and the actors even now learning their parts.

'But did you have to tell her that? Couldn't you have said the woman died of the flux?' Exasperation showed in his constant pacing.

'Impossible!' Kit strove to keep his temper. 'Would I have breathed a word of it if there had been any other way? I'm afraid you underestimate the tittle-tattle of servants, and Knyvett somehow got wind of it. Rumours are flying, believe me, and Hertford is in all probability on his way to our dear Queen right now with a mixture of fact and fiction in his saddlebags. Anyway, I think I did you a favour, didn't I? By lying! Saying she died in childbirth! How much worse would the truth have been?' Kit paused as Robert stopped his pacing to round on him.

'Why? What is the truth?' Robert had pricked his ears up at the mention of Hertford. What did Edward Seymour know about this? And whose side did this put Mister Hatton on? He had entertained ideas about Mary Seymour for as long as Robert could remember . . . Except, of course, that Kit didn't know that her name was really Seymour. Or did he? Even good friends had been known to become enemies overnight before now!

'Here.' Robert calmed himself and summoned up some practised charm. 'Sit down, and let me fill your cup. We'll unravel the tale over a bottle.'

And so at last, Mary's high and mighty attitude towards him was finally revealed to Kit. He whistled in amazement. Hertford's cousin! Tom Seymour's daughter! No wonder Elizabeth had . . .? Had she tried to recapture her youth? Without fear of producing bastards? And no wonder Mary would look no lower than a Knight of the Garter! Well, she had finally had her way. In a manner of speaking. How in hell's name had Robert persuaded her? He had obviously never suspected that Mary and Elizabeth . . . But then, why should he? The Queen was constantly surrounded by maids, just as many a man spent his time in the company of other men. Drinking. Jousting. Wrestling. It was not uncommon. And if the disgusting tale of perverted rape, as recounted by Robert, had any foundation in truth, it was no wonder that the girl had looked for her affection in gentler arms. Kit drained his cup. And then to end like that! Had it really been necessary to be so barbaric?

'When did you find all this out? That night . . .?'

Robert nodded. 'Aye. Thank God there aren't many such nights! I had to be certain that she wasn't a spy. From Elizabeth. I wasn't sure whether Meg Clifford had let the matter slip in an unguarded moment, or that one of Essex's cronies hadn't been sniffing round Durham House in the hope of implicating me in scandal.'

'So you seduced her. Was it easy?' Kit waited curiously for an answer.

'Well, I had to make sure of her after the things she had just witnessed. She was too deep in for me to ignore, but the shock she had suffered in seeing the sailor done away with gave me reason enough to comfort her, and after hearing of the way Will Darrel had abused her . . . it was a challenge. To make her eager for a man for the first time in her life.'

He smiled at Kit. 'Not the only time we have looked for something new to add to the enjoyment, is it?' Robert treated him to a lop-sided grin, reserved for his more intimate friends. Was that perhaps a hint of jealousy on Hatton's face?

'What was she like?' Kit remained subdued as his cup was refilled.

'In bed?' Robert shrugged his shoulders, playing down the novelty of the encounter. 'A woman. No more, no less. Less modesty than I expected in a virgin . . .'

Hardly surprising. Virgin, yes. Novice, no. But Kit kept those thoughts to himself.

'So she was not the Queen's spy? Then what was she doing in London when only days before she had been waiting on Elizabeth?'

'Ah,' Robert winked. 'It seems that she was looking for Meg Clifford, and knowing how things are between her and Tamworth, came to Leicester House to find her, hoping to get a potion from either her or Doctor Dee to bring her back into the Queen's favour. She felt threatened by Northampton's widow. Young Elin.'

That piece of information came as no surprise to Kit. 'And later? Did you know you had got her with child? Did she tell you?'

Robert shook his head. 'No. Frightened I should think. I had already warned her that I would deny everything if she began with accusations against me. I wanted that night with all its attendant pitfalls well and truly forgotten. Lettice was recovering, and Meg had gone into retirement for the season. I wanted no interference from Mary at that stage, especially as I was still juggling with the problem of Douglass and my son! Hell's teeth! I only have to look at a woman's crotch these days for her to begin swelling! No, it was months later when it dawned on me. Meg had been enquiring after Mary, the two of them being friends, and Elizabeth said she had gone to visit her old nurse at Littlecote Manor. Well! Would she really choose to go to that place unless she had something to hide and nowhere else to find assistance? No doubt she was hoping to be relieved of her burden as Lettice was. Old Elizabeth Fytton was well versed in that kind of thing, according to Meg.'

'Then why wasn't she? It would have been simpler than . . .' Kit had no need to go on.

'The old woman was too old and feeble. I enquired of Meg who told me that she was well past seventy, and the last time she had visited the old crone herself she had realized that there was nothing more to be learnt there. She lived in a world of her own, thanks to the potions and tinctures with which she dosed herself. I began to wonder. If she had not been able to rid herself of the child, if indeed that was the reason for her prolonged absence, then what could be done about it?' Robert leaned towards Kit. 'What could I have done? I couldn't have her returning with another squalling bundle to infuriate Elizabeth. My only hope was Darrel.'

'Aye. Darrel.' Had it been anyone but Darrel the child could have been lost amongst the peasantry and nothing more thought of it. But that would not be Darrel's style. The man was not only perverted. He was inhuman. 'Then what were your orders?' Kit knew that Robert had murdered in his time. But another son! Surely even he wouldn't stoop to that a second time!

'Tamworth got to Littlecote in the middle of a furious storm, and Mary was already in childbirth. And not an easy delivery, by all accounts. A midwife had been brought from a distant village to attend and she would probably have taken the child away with her. But for Tamworth arriving when he did! He showed Darrel my seal and swore that he would meet a sorry end if a word of the night's events were ever even whispered abroad. He was also given assurance that if he proved himself a friend, then he would not lack friendship should he ever be in need. He was well paid for his silence and Tamworth was back the next day, not having stayed in the area for fear of starting unnecessary rumours.'

'Then you still don't know what happened?' Kit was glad he had drunk a good deal of

Robert's wine. He had uncovered a gruesome tale which didn't bear thinking about. But Robert should hear it! If Hertford was about to make an issue of the thing then it was as well to know the worst.

'He took Tamworth at his word. Removed all evidence entirely. Your son was born perfect. Pink and healthy and with as lusty a pair of lungs as anyone could wish for. Will Darrel soon put a stop to that. He was determined that the whole household would not be witness to the birth.' Kit took another gulp of wine, wiping his mouth on the back of his hand before continuing. 'To end its mewling for its mother's paps he . . . he threw the newborn child onto the blazing fire. And when it screamed the louder in its agony he calmly piled fresh wood around it to hurry the end.'

Robert had buried his face in his hands. What was Kit trying to do? Brutal it may have been, but the very fact that Darrel had gone even further than he had been ordered, and probably enjoyed every minute of it, meant that his lips would be sealed. Elizabeth would never have to face the truth, no matter what she might suspect. And what could not be proved against Robert, Elizabeth had a way of conveniently ignoring. Removing two of his three mistakes wasn't a bad average.

'Then he strangled Mary.' Kit waited for this new piece of information to sink in. 'And the old woman, Elizabeth Fytton, already at death's door after witnessing the child's distressing end, was bludgeoned. Her skull cracked like an eggshell, it was so thin.'

'Enough! I want no more details! It is done.' He eyed the empty bottle balefully. 'Tamworth! Another!'

It appeared as if by magic.

'And if it does come to trial? Even if, as you think, Darrel keeps his mouth shut and you are not implicated . . . You will have to see to it that he is not imprisoned for the murders or he may change his mind on the subject of silence.'

'John Popham owes me a favour. And Darrel, being more inclined to stableboys than women, will have no heirs. Our friend John will say the right thing for the prospect of becoming the owner of Littlecote Manor on the present squire's demise. You agree?'

Kit couldn't help smiling. Robert certainly knew how to handle his affairs. And his friends!

As though reading his thoughts, Robert raised his goblet in salute. 'Still friends?'

'Aye,' Kit grinned at him. A young law student coming to Court, innocent and naive couldn't have chosen a better model to study for craft and guile. 'Still friends.'

Christopher Hatton had survived the long initiation, and in the jostle for position, the perilous climb to success, the Court would find no-one harder or more unbending than the Squire of Holdenby.

*   *   *

An opal gleam of dewdrops clung to his boots as the moisture-laden grass licked around his ankles in the hazy dawn. Slowly and steadily, wrapped in a cloak of yesterday's memories, Sir Christopher Hatton, Lord Chancellor of England, Knight of the Garter, gained the crest of Coneybury Hill. Only the silence called to him as he thought of the two heavy slabs, side by side in the little church. Francis. And Thomas. Both his brothers had long since mouldered to dust and neither would have easily recognized the man who stood surveying lands magnificently embellished with that massive drain on his resources, Holdenby Palace. A man held in high esteem by so many at the Court of Queen Elizabeth. Such high esteem that his memory was already immortal, his friend Drake having taken Kit's cognizance in the naming of his ship, *The Golden Hind*; the first to circumnavigate the earth.

Events of recent years flitted through his mind, as though he watched his own performance on life's stage. He heard again the desperate pleadings of William Parry as he was sentenced to be hung, drawn and quartered. Only Kit's persistent threats of torture had gained the confession. There could be no mercy from Sir Christopher where the Queen had been threatened. He was her man entirely. Parry, along with other Catholics, would find no sympathy there. The man was not the boy. As Henry Percy, eighth Earl of Northumberland had realized to his cost. The verdict had been suicide. Only Kit knew the truth. And in the Babington trial! Fourteen men had been hung, drawn and quartered. And hung for the shortest time possible on Kit's orders, before they were disembowelled and mutilated, still alive and fully conscious of the atrocities being perpetrated on their screaming flesh. Catholics, every one. Hatton had proved his devotion to his sovereign and earned his reward.

An unexpected breath of breeze riffled the long grass, whispering in the stillness, resurrecting the ancient past. When he had been a simple, ignorant boy. Before life consumed him; hardened him; tempered him, like steel.

'You don't understand . . . You don't understand . . .'

Mary Shea's voice haunted him.

'I love you . . . I love you . . .'

Imagination playing tricks. He had come so far since those carefree days. So far. What would the gipsy girl have thought of her gallant knight today? The laugh which escaped him had an edge of bitterness. Had it been worth it?

'No, Mary Shea, I didn't understand. But there is always a price to pay. You should have listened to your father. You had the remedy in your hand.'

The whisper in the grass faded and died, and the morning sun slit the pearl-grey sky with a single shaft of light. And in the distance, a cock crowed.

'Father! Father!'

The past melted away as his daughter Elizabeth ran towards him through the morning mist.

'See! Mushrooms!' She took hold of his hand. 'Oh, Father! How long have you been standing here? You'll catch cold.' She tutted and fussed about him, chatting non-stop as they made their way home.

Nan Hobson smiled quietly to herself as Kit approached, his arm lovingly around his child's shoulders, pride and affection showing in his eyes as he looked down at her. If a swarm of insects was to swoop down and surround them, there was no doubt in her mind that he would make a great show of fending them off with his cap. Just as he had on a warm summer evening long ago. Nan saw a man others had forgotten. The real man hidden behind a protective armour of severity, using cruelty as a shield. England may have a harsh and inflexible Lord Chancellor, but when he came home to Holdenby his family could still find, buried deep inside the courtier, the man they loved.